HAROLD'S
TAIL

HAROLD'S
TAIL

— *written and illustrated by* —

JOHN BEMELMANS MARCIANO

VIKING

VIKING
Published by Penguin Group
Penguin Young Readers Group,
345 Hudson Street, New York, New York 10014, U.S.A.
Penguin Books Ltd, 80 Strand, London WC2R 0RL, England
Penguin Books Australia Ltd, 250 Camberwell Road, Camberwell, Victoria 3124, Australia
Penguin Books Canada Ltd, 10 Alcorn Avenue, Toronto, Ontario, Canada M4V 3B2
Penguin Books (N.Z.) Ltd, 182-190 Wairau Road, Auckland 10, New Zealand

Published in 2003 by Viking, a division of Penguin Young Readers Group.

1 3 5 7 9 10 8 6 4 2

LIBRARY OF CONGRESS CATALOGING-IN-PUBLICATION DATA
Marciano, John Bemelmans.
Harold's tail / by John Marciano.
p. cm.
Summary: As a result of an experiment stripping the fur from his tail,
Harold the squirrel finds himself homeless and mistaken for a rat on the
unfamiliar streets of New York City.
ISBN 0-670-03660-9 (hardcover)
[1. Squirrels—Fiction. 2. Rats—Fiction. 3. New York (New
York)—Fiction.] I. Title.
PZ7.M328556Har 2003
[Fic]—dc21

Printed in U.S.A.
Set in Walbaum
Designed by Kelley McIntyre

The word "squirrel" comes from the Latin *sciurius*, which is derived from two Greek words, *skia* (shadow) and *oura* (tail), that put together mean "he who sits in the shadow of his own tail."

Table of Contents

HAROLD'S
TAIL

Introduction

This is a picture of my island. It's paradise, I think, and I'm a good one to judge because I know every inch of the place. There isn't a spot of earth I haven't dug up at one time or another, except for those spots where there are trees, and the trees I know best of all.

My name is Harold, and I am a squirrel. My island sits in the middle of another island, the island of Manhattan. Manhattan is an island surrounded by rivers; mine is an island surrounded by streets.

The name of my island is Straus Park, and it has an important history. There's a sign at the entrance of the park to tell you about it:

Straus Park: .44 acres

Straus Park is named in honor of Isidor and Ida Straus. The Strauses were passengers on the maiden voyage of the *Titanic*, the ship that was supposed to be unsinkable. On April 15, 1912, halfway from London to New York, the *Titanic* hit an iceberg. Although offered space on a lifeboat, Ida chose to stay with her husband aboard the sinking ship. The statue of Memory in Contemplation is dedicated to them, so that their love and loyalty will never be forgotten.

If you go past the sign and enter the park, you will see Memory at the end of the long walk in front of you. Memory is made of bronze, and she lies on her side, her lovely almond-shaped face lost in thought. A small fountain gurgles gently below her.

The walk between the sign and the statue is lined with park

benches and ginkgo trees. The ginkgo is unlike any other tree you will find. Its leaves are shaped like the wings of a small butterfly, and it has long slender branches that arc gracefully through the air. Despite its delicate beauty, the ginkgo is a hearty tree, which is why they are planted all along the streets of New York. In a city where other trees can't grow for lack of sunlight and room to spread their roots, the ginkgo gets along just fine.

As the sole squirrel inhabitant of Straus Park, I got along fine too. Before six months ago, I had never so much as set foot off my island. Why would I have? I had my .44 acres of paradise, and there I had always been safe, content, and happy, living in the shadow of my own tail.

Until. There wouldn't be a story without an "until."

CHAPTER 1
An Autumn Day

I woke with the sun. I lay in my nest high up in an elm tree and watched dawn glow from behind the tall apartment buildings on Broadway. In the other direction, the sky was still black. Morning in the east, night in the west, and me in between. I turned my head back and forth and watched the sun slowly win the sky, accompanied by the solitary sounds of early morning New York: a cab pulling away from a stoplight, the thud of bundled newspapers hitting the sidewalk, the lovely *whah-whah-*

whah of the garbage trucks making their rounds.

When it was day all over, I climbed down from the nest and had myself an early morning frolic. It was early November, but the weather was surprisingly warm. I hopped along the benches, onto the fence, up one ginkgo tree and over to the next one, and so on down the line. As always, I checked every bit of the island to make sure no one had littered or broken anything during the night. And then I raced around some more, just for fun.

Soon it was time for my appointments. People fed me all day long. Some of them came every day, at the same time, to the same place. My first appointment was with a subway conductor who, in his blue uniform, came to eat breakfast with me. He balled up pieces of bagel and dropped them to the ground for me, dipping the doughy little pebbles in cream cheese first, which I very much liked. What I really wanted was to try his coffee, which smelled wonderfully warm and welcoming as it steamed out of its blue-and-white cup. Unfortunately, he never offered me any.

Lots of people were in the park at this time of day, reading a newspaper or walking their dogs. Occasionally a dog lunged at me, but only for a foot or two—then it got yanked back by the throat. Imagine having to wear a leash! No wonder dogs bark and growl and chase animals that are allowed to live free. I'd be jealous too.

6

AN AUTUMN DAY

By late morning I had the park pretty much to myself. It was time to meet my favorite person, an older gentleman who wore a scarf and beret and carried a fine wood cane. First came a handful of peanuts. The man loved to watch me at work, breaking open the shells to get at the tasty nuggets inside. He laughed and clapped and shook all over and hollered "Wonderful!" and "Marvelous!" After a bit, he clucked to get my attention. Between his thumb and forefinger he was holding that most delicious, that most delightful, that most expensive of nuts, the macadamia. He tossed it to me and pushed himself up on his cane. "Good-bye squirrel," he said. "Good-bye my friend. Enjoy, enjoy!"

It wasn't the nuts that made Macadamia (as I called him) my favorite. It was that on the bitterest winter day, when not another soul came to the park, there Macadamia would be, waiting for me on a bench across from Memory, in the shadow of a tall ginkgo tree.

My favorite thing to do in the afternoons was to race long the treetops. From branch to branch I went, the thiner the better. The thinner ones drooped satisfyingly under ıy weight, lower and lower the longer I stayed on, to spring ack suddenly when I hopped off. Or I touched them so ently and briefly that they didn't move. It was like I was ınning on air, dancing in the sky—flying, almost.

Tired, I made my way down one of the long ginkgo ranches that hung over the sun-dappled statue of Memory. 'he leaves rustled like thousands of golden butterflies held ı place by tiny leashes. A few broke free and flapped a ıort but brilliant flight to the ground. I leapt down into the ıp of Memory and curled up in the crook of her hip. With ıe side of me warming on the bronze, the other in the sun, ıd my full belly warming me up inside, I slipped into appy dreams.

The sound of kids getting out of school woke me up. ome older folks were out too, with pistachios and almonds ıd sunflower seeds galore. I ate myself sick and spent the ıst of the afternoon burying the leftovers in different locaons around the island. Not that I needed them for later— ll through the winter there was plenty of food—but I'm a ıuirrel and I'm supposed to bury nuts. It's instinct, so I eally have no choice in the matter. (Plus I love the feeling f dirt between my claws.)

Finally, I did a little housework. I brought up some soft ıoss to cushion the nest with, and shredded a little bark ɔ put on top. I was very proud of my nest, how tightly ɔgether I had woven the thin ginkgo branches of the outer wall. It sat in the elbow of an elm tree, above the top of the honey locusts and ginkgos, up among the windows o the buildings that surrounded Straus Park. I liked th thought that in New York both people and I lived in nest in the sky, and I wondered if Macadamia could see my ne from his.

I got a visit from Terrence, a seagull who was fond o wandering over from the Hudson River. It was from hir I learned about the world beyond my island, abou Brooklyn and Queens, which are on Long Island, abou Staten Island and the ferry that goes there, about th great ships that are like floating islands, and about New Jersey, which is not an island, and a horrible place, according to Terrence. "Not a spot fit for squirrels or seagulls."

I would want every detail of the places he had seen. I'd ask him questions about other things too, like what did he know about the *Titanic*? "Well, if it was even bigger than the ships I have seen, then I'm not surprised it sank," he said. Once, I asked Terrence if h was a pigeon.

"Me? A pigeon!" Terrence said, horrified. "Well, we'r all birds, I suppose, but outside of that we have *nothing* i common. They are a lower class of species entirely. Pigeor have lice, they eat garbage, they can't float—in fact, the can't even walk, they waddle. And besides," Terrence adde with his beak in the air, "pigeons are idiots."

"It's true," I had to admit. "When you meet a pigeon, they don't have an awful lot to say."

That night, Terrence was tired of my questions. He asked, "Why do you care, Harold? You've never so much as crossed the street. Don't you wonder what's going on in the city around you, behind the windows, on the other side of the block? Don't you want to visit Central Park? Or Grant's Tomb? Riverside Park is only a block away and it's a haven for squirrels."

"No, thank you very much," I said. "This little island park suits me just fine. It has everything I need, everything I want." Terrence flew off into the setting sun. I pulled my tail over my body as a blanket and drifted off to sleep, to dream of the strange and frightening places that lay beyond the fences of Straus Park.

CHAPTER 2
Please Don't Litter

While making my morning rounds the next day,
noticed that one of the orange wire garbage baskets ha
been knocked over. Trash was spilled everywhere. I hoppe
over to investigate and was horrified to discover that a snak
had entered my island paradise.

It was, to be fair, a rather small snake. And then
moved closer and realized it wasn't a snake at all. It was
hairless tail, attached to the rather hairy rump of a rat. A
enormous, probably diseased, common street rat, who wa

licking the cream cheese off an old bagel wrapper. The cream cheese smelled rancid and had been soaked through with coffee. I felt sorry for the poor unfortunate creature—eating garbage!—but something had to be said.

"You there! Rat! I'm sorry, you've had your fun, now it's time for you to move on."

I'll never forget that hideous face turning toward me. The snout was smeared with cream cheese, crooked whiskers dripped coffee, and two front teeth hung down long and yellow. The rat rose on his back legs so he towered over me. My heart came up into my throat.

"Are you talking to *me*?" he said, pointing at himself. I was scared stiff, unable to speak. He leaned closer. "I said, are you talking to *me*?"

"Y-y-yes," I said, and gulped hard.

"You think you can tell me what to do?"

"Well, n-n-no, not in general, but I can tell you that a lot of people work hard to make this a nice little park, and—"

"Are you threatening me? You think I'm afraid of you?" The rat's eyes narrowed to slits. "You flouncy little squirrel, you."

"No, I don't mean to—I just—you probably didn't see the signs. That say not to litter? Maybe you don't know how to read—not to suggest you can't—which would be OK too—but, well, it might be best if you just moved on."

The rat moved so close I could feel his horrible breath on my face. "Listen up. You can't tell me what to do, not you or your signs. You think you're better than me, is

what it is," he said, poking me in the chest with a claw. "Well let me tell you something, flouncy boy, you ain't no better than me."

"I'm sure you're right," I said, trying to be polite.

"Darn right I'm right. You squirrels are all the same. Burying your nuts! Heaven forbid some other rodent so much as sniffs your leftovers." He folded his arms. "Yeah, you ain't no better than me. In fact, the only difference between you and me is that fluffy tail of yours."

"Oh, please!" I burst out laughing. "While it's true, I do have the better tail, do you honestly believe that's the only difference between the two of us? Take a look at yourself: your coat is grimy, you smell bad, you're out of shape and—no offense—your personality leaves a little something to be desired."

Now it was the rat's turn to laugh. "Oh ho ho that's rich! You think *you* have a good personality? Let me tell you something: your personality is your tail. Why, if I had that tail to shake and fluff, I'd be living out here in the sun all fat and happy too. In fact, if we switched tails I bet every person in this park would think you were the rat and I was the squirrel.

"That's ridiculous!" I said.

"Well if it's so ridiculous," he said smiling, "then you'll have no problem with a little experiment."

CHAPTER 3

The Broadway Barbershop

I was on one corner of 106th Street, and the rat (whose name, I had come to learn, was Sidney) was on the other. I had never crossed a street before, and you might as well have asked me to walk across the Hudson River or climb the sky to the clouds.

"Come on, flouncy boy," the rat yelled to me across the street. "See how the other half lives!" A white light on the sign above him was commanding me to WALK.

"I'm coming, I'm coming," I said. "Don't rush me." I walked to the edge of the crosswalk and looked one way,

hen the other, then back and forth and back and
orth. There were no cars to be seen. The sign
bove Sidney began to flash in orange letters
ONT WALK.

"What are you waiting for?" Sidney
elled.

"The sign says not to walk!" I shouted.

"This is New York—no one pays attention to
hose things!" he hollered back. "What's the matter,
ou never crossed a street before?"

"Of course I have," I lied. "It's just the sign!" But
hen it said WALK again.

I held my breath and raced across the street as fast
s I could.

I stopped and turned around. I'd never seen Straus Park
om the outside before. It looked so strange from this per-
ective that it was hard to even recognize. And to see the
uildings from the sidewalk! They seemed to go as high as
he sky itself.

By the time I caught up with Sidney he was stopped in
ont of an old storefront. A sign hung on the door said
CLOSED. Outside stood a thick wooden pole painted
with white and red stripes, although the paint
was mostly faded away. I perched on top
of it while Sidney went up the door. He
was a terrible climber.

"Where are you trying to get to?" I asked.

"The transom—*hoowh hoowh*—" he panted,
"window."

There was a small rectangular window above the doo
that was tilted open. Sidney pulled himself up to the win
dow and slid awkwardly across it before scurrying down th
other side of the door like he was falling. He waved for m
to come in.

Breaking and entering? What would this rat get m
into next? I should have run away, but instead I jumpe
from the pole to the transom window, glided across i
and walked headfirst down the door. "Show-off," Sidne
muttered.

The inside of the Broadway Barbershop was like nothin
I had ever imagined. The floor was a mosaic of white and blu
tiles, and there were two rows of enormous porcelain chai
with red leather seats and headrests. The walls were line
with mirrors and marble countertops, upon which sat gleam
ing metal instruments, bottles of different-colored liquid
and all kinds of tubes and tins.

I jumped up to the counter and was lost in lookin
around when Sidney came at me with a pair of scissor
"What are you going to do with those!" I asked.

"Well, flouncy boy, I'm gonna cut the hair off of you
tail and glue it onto mine, and then we'll see how much di
ference there is between the two of us."

"Oh no you're not!" I said.

"What, are you *scared*?" he asked. He opened the sci
sors with a slow scrape of the one blade against the oth
and—*snip!*—snapped them shut. "Scared to find out tha
your precious people friends only love you because
your tail? Scared to find out that underneath that gra

uff you're just a rat like me? Poor little flouncy squirrel,
should've known you'd chicken out."

"I'm not afraid," I said. "It's just I feel sorry for you, that
ou're about to find out a tail has nothing to do with any-
ing."

Sidney's crooked whiskers angled up as he smiled. "OK
en. Turn around and hold still." Scissors open, Sidney
ied to angle my tail fur in between the blades.

"You sure you know what you're doing?"

"Sure I'm sure," Sidney said. "I read a manual once." I
ecided not to look.

Sidney kept me waiting and waiting, and I was getting
ore and more nervous. What if he cut off my entire tail?
wasn't too late to back out. I loved my beautiful—

Sssssssssnnnnniiiiip!

I could hear, and I swear, even *feel* the individual hairs
eing cut. Finally Sidney said, "OK, that's it for these," and
e scissors clanked against the marble countertop.

I turned to inspect my tail. It wasn't so bad. There was
ill hair on it, just short and uneven. More upsetting was
e pile of hair on the counter. It had always been a part of
e; now it was just a mess in some strange place.

The silence of the barbershop was interrupted by a loud
osh! Sidney was pressing down on the top of a can that
as spraying out heaps of white foam. Having formed a
all mountain of the stuff, Sidney scooped up a handful
lather and rubbed it over my tail, which I have
say felt rather nice. He kept
ding lather until my tail was

19

bigger and fluffier than it had ever been.

Sidney reached into this foamy white cloud, grabbed th
end of my tail, and yanked it straight. He picked up a stubb
stainless steel instrument in his other hand. "This is a razo
he said, wagging it at me. "It's sharp, so unless you like blee
ing, I suggest you don't move." I braced myself, but in a fe
sweeps up my tail he was done. "OK flouncy, time to take
look at the new you."

I turned and took my tail into my paws. My tail! Whe
had it gone? I had never seen my skin before, and now sk
was all there was.

Sidney collected my tail hair into a neat pile and open
a tin marked TOUPEE GLUE. He stuck a fistful of hair in th
glue and then stuck it on his tail. At first he looked silly, b
the more he put on, the more he looked like someone els

I couldn't bear to watch directly, so I watched in the mi
ror. I saw the two of us, side by side, the rat and the squirr
and I couldn't believe the one on the right was me.

CHAPTER 4
The Experiment

We were back in the park, hiding behind the ivy-covered trunk of a ginkgo tree watching Macadamia. The tail doesn't matter, I kept telling myself. This is my old friend, he'll know who I am. He probably won't even notice the tail.

"Are you waiting for it to grow back? Let's go."

"I'm going, I'm going," I said. As I walked out from behind the shiny green shield of the ivy, I felt like I was leaping for a branch I wasn't sure I could reach.

Macadamia burst into a smile as soon as he saw me.

Relief! Then his happy expression evaporated. He looked me over. Was that concern on his face? Was he wondering *What happened to my poor friend's tail?* Without thinking I flicked my tail twice. For a squirrel it's impossible not to do—it's like you blinking your eyes.

Suddenly, I found myself on my back, swatted there by the business end of Macadamia's cane. "Get away! Off with you!" Macadamia pounded the ground with his cane. "You rat!"

I raced back behind the tree, where I found Sidney doubled over in laughter. "D-did you see the way he, the way he—he—he—ha ha ha, ho ho ho!"

The humiliation burned at me. "Oh yes, it's very funny, ha ha, ho ho," I said. "He needs eyeglasses, a man his age."

"Oh, I think he can see perfectly."

"Well let's see you try, then," I said.

"Ah, quit rushing me!" Sidney said, and his good humor disappeared.

The rat made his way out toward Macadamia's bench looking every bit the impostor he was. He slunk, with no spring in his step, and dragged his new tail flat along the ground. Everything about him was exceedingly ratlike.

Macadamia eyed Sidney with the same confusion and scrutiny he had shown me. Thankfully this sham was about to be exposed. Macadamia would realize that I had been mugged of my tail fur.

In desperation, Sidney flicked his tail. He didn't do it like a squirrel, though; he did it like a bug had crawled onto his tail and he was trying to shake it off.

A smile came to Macadamia's lips, and then a hiccup of a laugh. "Well, who are *you*?" Macadamia said. "An awfully big squirrel, it would seem."

It was agony watching Macadamia reach into his bag. He flung a fistful of peanuts up into the air. For a moment, they hung suspended like leaves on a tree. As they rained down on Sidney, a look of ecstasy swept over the rat's face. It must have been the happiest moment of Sidney's life, and for an instant I felt happy for him.

I will spare you the horrifying details of the rest of the day, except to say that the scene with Macadamia repeated itself with my every appointment.

I did no frolicking, and I went to take my afternoon nap up in the nest. But how could I sleep? I didn't bother coming down the whole afternoon. It

would've been unbearable to watch Sidney gobble up mor
of my nuts and fruit and bread crusts, or to hear anyone els
shriek at the sight of me. I busied myself fussing around th
nest, rearranging the moss and shredded bark and feather
but it didn't take my mind off any of it.

"My goodness but you are a hungry fella," Macadami
had said before he left. "Usually, I only give my squirrel on
macadamia nut, but I think I have to give you three o
four."

Oh Macadamia, I would have believed it of anyone els
but you? Was my bright fluffy tail really all that mattere
His words kept repeating in my head: *You rat! Off with yo
you rat!*

Sidney started to climb the elm tree. Now I'd have t
listen to him gloat. I made up
my mind to ignore him.

"Hoo, Daddy!" Sidney said,
huffing and puffing. "I think I ate too
much, but *whih-whoo!*" he whistled.
"Look at the view from up here, boy.
You can see the whole neighborhood.
Choice digs!"

My cheeks burned, but I
bit my tongue.

"You squirrels sure
have the life—or should
I say, I, squirrel, sure
have the life. You, my friend,
had better make yourself scarce. As in: Beat it. Scram

Sidney sniffed and thrust his nose up in the air. "Truth is, we don't like your kind around here. In fact, all the talk down on the benches is about the rat problem. I wouldn't be surprised if the exterminator made a little visit tomorrow."

"The what?" I said, unable to keep quiet.

"Oh yeah, the exterminator," Sidney said, leaning over me. "He's the one that puts down the poison. That's how people deal with you rats when you show up in their parks. Don't worry, though—you're only sick for a couple of days before you kick the bucket."

With the word "kick," Sidney slapped me hard on the shoulder, knocking me against one side of the nest. He stretched out on his back, fluffed up some feathers behind his head, and put his legs up on the side. "Com-for-ta-ble!"

It was too much to bear—Sidney in *my* nest, wearing *my* tail, his belly full of food meant for *me*. I made a decision: I had to get out of Straus Park.

I climbed out of the nest, hopped off the elm tree, and took one final turn around my island. The ginkgos, the honey locusts, the benches, Memory; would I ever see them again? How long does it take a tail to grow? A week? A month? A year? I'd die, away from this beautiful place for so long. Maybe there was some way I could stay—but for what? More humiliation and betrayal and getting beaten with a cane? There was nowhere to hide. I'd be poisoned or starve to death. I had no choice but to go.

I walked away into the setting sun, my naked tail dragging along behind me. I couldn't help but flick it, and every time I did, it shamed me. I promised myself I wouldn't look back, but I did. A wind off the river rushed over me, and a moment later reached Straus Park and gave the ginkgo trees a shake. The golden butterflies rained down, and they broke my heart.

CHAPTER 5

The Importance of a Pretty Bow

Where was I to go? I wasn't sure. I headed down the middle of the sidewalk along 107th Street, shivering without my tail fur. Coming toward me was a young couple, laughing and holding hands. The girl stopped dead, her eyes opened wide. She shrieked.

I leapt, terrified. "Ah! Ah! Ah!" Her screams came in loud hysterical bursts. The man steeled himself to do something about me but I saved him the trouble and ducked under a gate that led into an alley.

"This city has got to do something about the rat problem," the girl said as they walked on.

I had to figure out a place to spend the night. Not the streets; they were too dangerous. Above me was a fire escape. Its ladder hung down to the gate. I climbed up as far as I could go—it felt good to be high. On the top landing sat a big clay pot, still half full of dirt from some plant that had died. I curled up inside.

I lay there like I was asleep, as if pretending to sleep would make it happen. When I woke up I'd realize this had all been a bad dream. But I couldn't sleep, so I just hoped for the night to end. Maybe by morning some tail hair would have grown back.

Finally, the distant wail of a garbage truck announced it was morning, and I thought about how the subway conductor in the blue suit might be meeting Sidney for the first time right now, feeding him little pebbles of my bagel. I felt a pain in my stomach. Was it hunger? I couldn't tell, I'd never been hungry before. But if that's what it was, I didn't like hunger one bit.

I inspected my tail. I began at the tip and carefully worked my way back, checking the underside as well, but it was the same everywhere. Bald.

It was dark and cold on the fire escape. Sunlight, however, seemed to be streaming behind the town house across the alley. I climbed down to investigate.

In back of the town house was a wall. I scaled it and saw that there were small gardens in back of the buildings. I was a little world unto itself. It had never occurred to me that a block was hollow inside—I thought the rear of one building met the rear of the next.

I hopped along the fences that separated the gardens until I reached the farthest one, the only one getting sun. Where the sun hit the ground lay a longhaired cat on its back. It had a blue bow around its neck. There was a noise coming from somewhere that sounded like the motor of a car. I climbed down and slowly, carefully, approached the cat. The sound got louder—it appeared to be coming from the cat itself. Maybe this was the sound of a dead cat, since it hadn't moved or made any sign of noticing me, although I was now right in front of its head. It was eerie, that sound and nothing else, everything so still, here in this world of hidden gardens.

"Uh, excuse me. Mr. Cat?" I said softly.

The sound abruptly stopped. One eye opened, slowly, as if doing so took a tremendous effort. A shiny yellow eyeball was revealed, with a thin black slit of a pupil that grew wider as it focused on me.

"And what, pray tell, are you?" The cat sounded so displeased that I took a step back, even though he had moved

nothing but that one eye. "A small rat? A large mouse? You have a lot of nerve, certainly, waking a sleeping cat."

"Oh, I'm sorry," I said. "I'm a bald squirrel—well, my tail's bald, but—"

"Whatever you are, I suppose it's my job to chase you, but the sun is too delicious right now. You know, the sun is only in this garden for an hour or two a day, so these are precious minutes, my friend. *Precious* minutes," he repeated.

"Well, perhaps I could stay for a little bit? While the sun is nice?"

"Oh no, that's not possible. What if someone were to come home and see that I had allowed vermin such as yourself into the yard? Then what? They might take away my pretty bow. This is my favorite bow, you know. It makes me look all the more handsome. I also have a green bow, but that one clashes with the flecks of green in my eyes, which are my most extraordinary feature. Most cats have uninteresting eyes that are either plain yellow or plain green, but mine are both, which is much better." Pleased with what he had said, the cat closed his eye and the sound returned.

"What is that sound?" I asked. "Coming out of you, I mean."

"You must be talking about my purr. Yes it is very loud—many people say it is the loudest purr they have ever heard. Also, it is deep and resonant, like a cello. I purr when I am happy, which is most of the time, except for when I get a can of Fisherman's Catch for dinner. I don't care for seafood." He swished his tail once at the thought of it. "Sliced Turkey, now there's a can of cat food. But do you see what you're doing

You're making me hungry, so now I suppose I'll have to get up and go out of the sun to eat some kibble."

Food—the very mention of it! The pain returned, and now I knew it must be hunger. "Perhaps, if you don't mind, could try some of your kibble?"

The purring abruptly stopped and both eyes opened, not slowly. "You certainly may not! If you were to so much as try I'd have to kill you, and don't think I wouldn't. Why, I imagine one less bald squirrel in the world would be a welcome thing. In fact, I might even be rewarded with a new bow. Which brings us back to the point, my bow. Don't you think it looks well on me?" His eyes closed again but he continued talking, and I slipped away.

"I suppose there are prettier bows in the world but somehow I doubt it. . . ."

CHAPTER 6
Riverside Park

I was watching the sky, back on top of the fire escape.
My heart leapt every time a bird passed overhead—was it
Terrence? Terrence would know what to do. Maybe he'd
even let me get on his back or grab his legs so that he could
carry me away to Long Island or Staten Island or one of
those other islands he had told me about. Then it hit me.
Riverside Park! It's a haven for squirrels, Terrence had said,
and only a block away. Why did it take me so long to think
of it? I had never met any other squirrels before, but surely

the ones in Riverside would let me stay with them.

I exited the alley and hit the sidewalk at full hop. I could see it immediately, Riverside Park, right at the end of the block. From up the hill, it didn't look that much different from Straus Park. But at the end of the street, the view opened. It was beyond belief. To the left, to the right, nothing but trees, as far as the eye could see!

I was so mesmerized that I didn't see that I had crossed into the middle of Riverside Drive—tires screeched and a car jerked wildly to avoid me. I turned back, but another car whizzed by the other way. The lights had all gone green. DONT WALK! DONT WALK! screamed signs in every direction. Vehicles were whipping by in both directions. I was trapped between two yellow lines, completely frozen, except for my wildly beating heart.

Then, a break in traffic. If I'd thought about it I wouldn't have moved—but I didn't think, I didn't even look, I took off running and didn't stop until I was safely on a tree.

Out of breath, my heart still pounding, it took me a minute to notice the tree. Such a tree! What kind was it? I raced up the branches, which curved around at impossible angles. I hopped onto a tree beside it, a ginkgo, but one five times the size of any ginkgo I had ever been on. And that was nothing—the next tree was a skyscraper! I could circle the trunk of any tree in Straus Park and see my tail on the other side, but I could get lost circumnavigating this one.

Then there was a tree that had leaves as big as me, and smooth, white bark that was dappled gray. Another one had jagged leaves and spiky green fruit hanging on its branches. I was dizzy. Who knew there were this many different types of trees in the whole world? Why hadn't I come sooner? I had a feeling I was going to like it here.

A familiar sound pierced the air. On the trunk of the next tree was a squirrel cracking open a nut. It was odd. I had never seen another squirrel before—it was like looking at Straus Park from the other side of the street.

A second squirrel raced up the tree. The first one grabbed the nut in his mouth and ran away to the other side of the trunk. The second squirrel chased him. Around and around they went, the tail of one disappearing as the head of the other came into view.

"Hello!" I called. Both squirrels stopped dead and looked up at me, their mouths agape. The nut dropped. "Hello?" I repeated.

The squirrels suddenly began chattering in a foreign language, full of fast clicks and twittering, *cukcukcuk*. They raced up the trunk and vanished into the thicket of branches above, *cukcukcuk*ing all the way.

I was disappointed. I sat there on the branch, thinking about what I would say if they came back, when the branches above me rustled. Out jumped one squirrel, then a second, and a third. These squirrels were different. The first had a reddish tail and face, the second, blond markings, and the third was completely black. And they were much bigger.

"Hello," I said. "I'm Harold."

The red squirrel ran along the branch above me, heading toward me, then over me. The blond followed, but stopped directly above where I was sitting.

"I—I was hoping maybe I could stay here for a while," I said. "In Riverside."

The black one leapt onto the very tip of the branch I was on. It sagged under the extra weight. He approached me slowly. Coming on the branch the other way was the red squirrel.

"You know, if you guys don't mind a—a guest."

Their tails flicked ominously.

Vnk-vnk-vnk! the blond one went. I had no idea what it meant, but the tone was menacing.

Vnk-vnk-vnk! The red made the same sound. Then, in a thick accent, "No escape!"

The black gnashed his teeth.

"So you guys don't want co-company." I tried to smile. "That's OK. I'll just be going then."

"No escape!" the red one repeated. He and the black were now practically upon me. The branch had gotten very small. Since the way up was blocked by the blond squirrel, I looked for a branch below me. Nothing, except the trunk, very far away. What were they going to do to me? I looked into the night-dark eyes of the black squirrel, just a whisker's length away, and I didn't want to find out. I leapt . . .

And I fell, and fell, drifting toward the trunk as the ground rushed up. Straining, I reached out with my front legs, my claws began to scrape the bark, then to dig in, bits of bark flew, I was slowing down—it hurt, but finally I got a hold and was under control, hopping down as fast I could, and then, *stop!* There was a gray squirrel at the base of the tree, his tail flicking madly. *Vnk-vnk-vnk!* he yelled up. "No escape!"

I tried circling the tree, but he anticipated my every move. I turned to go back up. The black, the blond, and the red were coming down, fanning out. I backed up, moved to the side, but I was surrounded.

Vnk! Vnk! the black squirrel said. "No escape for you."

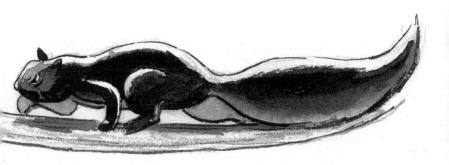

CHAPTER 7

The Grand Council

I was in a nest atop the tallest tree in Riverside Park.
can't imagine how it had been built, resting as it did be
tween two slight branches. Not that it had been built well; i
had no lining and was loosely woven with rough branche
that left wide gaps, through which I could see the red, blond
and black squirrels, perched in the other branches of the
tree's crown. How long would they keep me in this jail?

Around me was nothing but sky. Gray and black cloud
passed across each other like smoke. The nest swayed, the

the wind picked up and sent it careening. The nest felt like it might blow off the tree like the hat from a head.

As afternoon faded into night, the black squirrel climbed up as far as the edge of the nest, stuck his head over, spit out an acorn, and climbed back down. I gnawed on the shell but couldn't eat. Starving though I was, my stomach was too queasy from the motion.

In the distance I could see the lighted windows of the apartment buildings—people, warm and safe. Those lights had never seemed so far away. I didn't even think about my tail; I just hoped I'd make it out of Riverside Park alive.

Only when it got light did I feel a little better. Why is the day always less scary than the night?

"Come down, interloper!" rose the angry voice of one of my jailers. "Now!"

I carefully climbed down and was escorted away, the blond and red squirrels in front, the black following behind me.

"Where are we going?" I asked.

They chattered amongst themselves. "The justice!" the red one said.

We went from one tree to the next, deeper and deeper into the park, down toward the river. The trees here were so close together and so thick with branches it was impossible to see out. There was scattered chattering. I saw lumps in the trees ahead—nests, enormous leafy nests—with heads poking out, slowly turning to watch me pass, eyes inside the trees even, from hollowed-out dens in the trunks. The chattering was now a loud, low rumble, and

ere were squirrels everywhere, on every branch, above, elow, and in front of me.

In the dark heart of the forest was a tree so thick its anches were like the trunks of other trees. The black uirrel led me onto one of these branches, put me so my ick was against the main trunk. The branch split into ven as it rose. On each was a gray squirrel. They were der, with shaggy faces and severe expressions. The owd grew louder. I looked for a way to escape, but it was peless.

The central squirrel rose up. "Silence! Silence!" All eyes rned to him. "In my capacity as Head of the All-Powerful stices, I hereby designate as begun this meeting of the rand Council of the Brotherhood of Squirrels in the Great omain of Riverside Park, the Kingdom of the Treetops. day we will decide the fate of the bald interloper who vaded our fair park yesterday evening." There was a burst evil-sounding chatter.

The head justice, who had an abundant array of hiskers, rested again on his branch and turned his atten- on to me. "Explain yourself, bald one. Why are you here?"

"Well, I came here to—"

"Louder!"

I cleared my throat. "I, uhm, came here because I had to. had to go somewhere, because I can't stay home anymore."

"And home, where is your home?"

"It's the park up the hill," I said, and there was a sud- en frenzy of clicks and chattering. The head justice him- lf seemed taken aback.

"Are you saying you are from the great land of sin? Tha you are from Central Park? Why didn't you identify your self?"

"A spy! Spy!" came calls from the crowd.

"No, no, no," I said. "This is all a big misunderstandin I'm not from Central Park, I'm from Straus Park. It's onl a block or so away."

The head justice looked confused. "And why have never heard of this Straus Park?"

"Well, I'm the only squirrel there, or I was. I had t leave because there was this rat, you see, and he cut off m

tail fur so he could have it for himself, and then the people in the park thought I was the rat, so they chased *me* away."

The head justice gave me a harsh look. "And you expect us to believe this preposterous story?"

One of the other justices said, "I think it's more likely that *you* are the rat!"

"It wouldn't be the first time one of them had tried to take to the trees!" another added.

"That would explain why he speaks the barbaric language of the streets and can't understand the simplest clicks or chattering," the head justice said. "However, I think it far more likely that he is suffering from mange. I'm one of the few old enough to remember the last out-break. It starts with clumps falling out of the tail, yes, but then it moves on, to the fur on the body and eventually to the brain, where it ends in madness and certain death!"

"Please, you must believe me," I said, speaking not just to the head justice but to the entire crowd. "I don't have any diseases, really, it was a rat! I just wanted a place to stay."

"I think that we have heard enough," the head justice said. "What say my fellow justices?"

"I say he's a spy!" the squirrel to the far left said. "Central Park is full to bursting with squirrels—they want to take over our trees!"

"I agree," said the justice standing next to him.

The one closest to the head justice said, "No, I say the poor wretch is suffering from an advanced case of mange."

"I say he's diseased *and* he's a spy," said the justice on the far right. "You know the habits of those filthy Central Parkers."

"I think it's obvious that he's a rat," said the next squirrel, who was all gnarled and hunched over. "Look at his tail, not a hair on it. And those unmistakably beady eyes! Why, I can see him rifling through garbage cans now."

"He does look every inch a rat," said the last one, who was particularly sinister looking.

There came again the evil hum of the crowd while the head justice leaned back on his haunches. He pinned his ears back while he considered my fate. "I want us to remember how lucky we are here in Riverside Park, with its magnificent trees that provide for our every need. We must hold on to what we have, maintain our borders. It matters not whether this alien be a spy, a rat, or infected—in all cases my ruling is the same: expulsion!"

"Expulsion! Expulsion!"

As the three guards reappeared to lead me away, the scattered cries, chattering, and clicking gave way to a steady chant: "OUT OUT OUT OUT OUT OUT OUT!" The chant faded as we made our way out of the forest and into the light. We went from tree to tree up the hill until we reached Riverside Drive. The three squirrels stood as a wall while I crossed to the other side, grateful to be alive. The streets of New York looked suddenly inviting.

CHAPTER 8
One Angry Bird

I was hiding in the branches of a scrawny honey locust tree, nibbling on some seeds, trying to hold off starvation. Unfortunately, honey locust seeds taste like cardboard. A man in a hooded sweatshirt passed below me eating a slice of pizza. Waddling alongside him on the sidewalk was a pigeon. The pigeon would waddle as fast as he could, and once he was a few steps in front of the man he would stop and gaze up longingly. The man would pass, and the pigeon would repeat the procedure.

"You really want some pizza, huh?" the man said to the pigeon.

The pigeon batted his wings.

The man tore off half the crust and tossed it at the bird's feet. "Here," he said. "I don't like the crust anyway."

The pigeon furiously pecked away at it. Peck peck, swallow, peck peck, swallow, and the crust danced around the sidewalk. As soon as the man had passed me, I hopped down from the basket and approached the pigeon.

"Excuse me, pigeon, sir," I said. "Could you spare a bit of that crust?"

The pigeon looked at me with a mixture of surprise and fury. He grabbed the crust in his beak and waddled away from me, double speed, but he hadn't gotten far when from the sky descended a flock of pigeons—five, ten, twenty, more—wings beating and beaks striking, all aiming for that crust.

The original pigeon did his best to keep the crust away, turning his head this way and that, but one of his attackers managed to tear away a good chunk of the crust, a couple of others got beakfuls, and then I lost sight of the poor bird in a swarm of gray, black, and white feathers.

A few pigeons flew away from the gaggle with small stolen prizes, each of them pursued in turn by a few hopeful thieves. Slowly, the struggling mass began to break apart until there were just a few pigeons poking at white specks in the cement, hoping one of them might be a crumb.

Out from these last dejected few marched one angry bird, coming straight for me.

"Thanks a lot!" the pigeon said.

"Did I do something wrong?" I said.

"*Did I do something wrong? Did I do something wrong?*" he mocked me. "Why, I had that crust all to myself before you came along and alerted the entire pigeon population of New York City!"

"Honestly, I don't see how——"

"You don't see! You don't see! Of course you don't see!  You don't know what it's like on these streets when you're a pigeon, fighting for every crumb. Do you have any idea how many millions of pigeons live in this city? How many? Do you? Millions of millions! Billions of millions! And every one of them is at war with every other one. We don't need rats coming out during the day for more competition."

"Actually, I'm a——"

"Actually, you're a dirty rotten rat, is actually what you are. And until night comes I suggest you hide yourself in whatever rat hole you came out of before I personally peck your eyes out. Remember: during the day, the streets are ours!" he yelled, and flew away.

CHAPTER 9

The Basement

It got cold. Wind bent the skinny honey locust backwards and whipped off the last of its remaining leaves. They collected in a pile against a stoop down the block. Unprotected, the tree and I both shivered. When I could take it no more, I hurried down the tree and behind some garbage cans chained to the front of a brownstone.

How much worse could my life get? I was cold and tired, starving and depressed, forgotten by my friends, replaced by a rat, rejected by cats and pigeons and even squirrels, and now I had to hold my nose because the garbage stank so badly.

But then I felt something wonderful, like a warm breath on my neck. Where was it coming from? I turned and walked along the edge of the building until I came to a window even with the ground and not much taller than me. It was boarded up, but there was a hole in the wood, round and perfect like it was there for a reason.

I stuck my head in the hole. It was too dark to see anything, but it felt like summer inside. It would be nice to sleep in there, but what if it was someone's apartment?

It didn't smell the way you'd think an apartment would, though—it smelled kind of like dirt. I climbed through the hole and carefully made my way down the wall on the other side.

It was a long way to the bottom and wonderfully hot down there. I couldn't tell if the floor was made of dirt or

ıst dirty, but I liked it either way. As my eyes began to adjust
» the darkness I could see shapes. There were boxes, lots of
oxes, but I didn't recognize anything else. Something was
ıumming. It sounded like a loud engine, and it was accom-
anied by the occasional clank, like one pipe hitting anoth-
ı. The first clank made me jump. I should have searched
round to make sure everything was safe, but I was tired, so
red, and it being all warm and dark made me even more
red. I curled up on the floor. It felt wonderful to be safe
nd warm . . . so wonderful . . . safe and . . . warm and . . .
nd . . . tired*ddd* . . .

Scratch, scratch.

I woke with a start. Somebody—something—was in the
oom.

"Who is it?" I said. "Who's there?"

Clank! Clank!

I looked for something moving in the darkness, tried
o decipher the shapes, now not just unfamiliar but
hreatening. There was still that humming too, and again:
Clank! Clank! I made for the window, slow steps, then
uicker ones, and then I felt *it*. Whatever it was, was right
n front of me, blocking my way. I slowly tried to move
round it, but it was right on top of me. I whirled, took a
tep back, and hit the wall. I was trapped. A wheezing
reath was blowing on me, a breath that smelled like a
otten tomato.

kkkkhmMPH! kkkkhmMPH! went the sound of wind
eing sucked in. I was petrified. Something cold and wet
ressed up against me.

kkkkhmMPH! it sniffed agai
"Smells like squirrels! What's squi
rels doing down in my nest?"
could see the horrible bea
now—it was some so
of rat, but monstrou
It had patches of f
missing, and a chunk o
of one ear, and crooked whiskers sprout∢
out of all parts of its head. And its eyes! They were cor
pletely white.

"Did you comes down here for me to eat you, squirrel
Its long claws were feeling me all over, my face, my stor
ach, my arms. "Beens a long time coming since I had n
some squirrels meat. But I remembers it well—it's a da
meat, stringy, a littles bit gamy for sure, but good eats."

The creature dug into my shoulders with its claws ar
tried to pull me toward it. I struggled, beat against its che
with my back legs, but it was so strong. So this was it, th
was how I was going to die: eaten alive by a rat monster
screamed as its decaying yellow teeth bit into my arm, ar
then—I went blind.

The blindness came from a sudden, explosive brightne
At first I thought it was the Light, the light that you s
when you die. But I didn't think your eyes would hurt li
this if you were dead. I shut them tight and that helped t
pain, but I wanted to watch what was happening so I blink
them very fast and I could see that the rat monster w
doing the same.

"C'mon Omar," came a voice from the other side of the room. "Lighten up on the little fella."

"Buh!" the rat monster said. "Turns off that light!"

"What's going on? Who is it?" I called.

"My name's King, and I'm the head of this little basement household. I see you've already met Omar." I could now see that King was another rat. He was hanging on to a long string that was connected to a lightbulb on the ceiling. "The question is, who are you?"

"I'm Harold," I said.

"Well, Harold," King said, "you are, without a doubt, the funniest looking rat I have ever laid eyes on."

"I am *not* a rat," I said, and immediately regretted my tone.

"What are you then, the world's biggest mouse?"

"He's squirrel," Omar said, grabbing my arm and sniffing it. *kkkkhmMPH!*

"Please!" I said, snatching it back.

"Don't worry, old Omar won't eat you. He'd like to, of course, but those teeth aren't good for much of anything these days."

"Well, that's comforting," I said.

"I brought this orange rind back for Omar, but since you're our guest, I'd like you to have it."

King placed the rind between me and him and it sat

there pathetically, all dry, hard, and smelly. I didn't move to take it or say a word until after it had become awkward.

"Well, thank you very much," I said. "But really, let Omar have it. He's obviously very hungry."

"Buh! If I can't have fresh squirrels meat, then I wants nothing."

"C'mon," King said, picking the rind back up and holding it under my nose. "Have some."

"I'm, uhm . . ." How could I put this politely? "I'm afraid it wouldn't agree with me."

"Agree with you?" King shrugged. "What do you mean? The orange rind doesn't have an opinion."

"But, it's, it's *garbage*."

"Exactly. Found it right in the garbage can next door." King held the rind up to his nose and took a good whiff. "Smell that flavor!" He took a bite out of it like a potato chip and chewed, *crunch crunch*. "So what's a squirrel like you doing with a tail like that?" King said, his mouth full.

I told King and Omar about my beautiful park and wonderful life and how a—pardon the expression—rat came along and wrecked it.

"By any chance," King asked, "did this rat go by the name of Sidney?"

"How'd you know?" I asked, shocked.

"Only Sidney," King said. "Oh well, at least he's OK. We were afraid something happened to him."

"The exterminator!" Omar said.

"I've heard," I said. We all nodded gravely.

"Someone needs to smack that rat around a little bit, knock some sense into him," King said. "Not a bad guy, Sidney, it's just he hates being a rat. Can you imagine that? I mean, I wouldn't be nothing else."

"I don't mean to be rude," I said, "but really?"

"Oh yeah. I mean, look at you, begging for your food, and then it just comes. It's too easy. Now me, I don't beg nobody for nothing—I work for a living. Hunting, collecting, scavenging—a rat earns what he eats, and that makes it taste better." King put an arm around me.

"And that's why it's great being a rat?" I asked.

"That and being able to scare the bejeezus out of anyone walking down the street."

"King, that would be what you'd like about being a rat," came a voice that floated down from above. Leaning into the hole in the window was a rat with her head resting on her arms. Her fur was light brown and she was so clean and pretty that I wondered if she even was a rat.

"Harold, may I introduce to you Amelia," King said, and gestured up to the window with a grand sweep of his arms.

"Hello there," she said.

"Hi," I said.

"My, but you're an interesting looking rat," Amelia said.

55

"Thank you," I said. "But actually, I'm not a rat."

"Not this again," King said. "Look, let's settle a couple things. One, we're all rodents here, so what's the difference who's a rat and who's a squirrel? Two, we've got plenty of room, so Harold, if you want to, you can bed down with us for as long as you like."

"You really should," Amelia said. "We have this wonderful boiler to keep us toasty warm." She pointed to a squat iron machine with gauges and handles all over it and pipes going up to the ceiling. "It's a little noisy, but not too bad."

If someone had asked me three days before, "Would you like to squat with a pack of rats in a basement?" I would've told them they were crazy. That night I was thrilled by the offer. "Yes. Thank you very much, I would," I said. "In fact I wouldn't mind getting some sleep right now. I haven't slept in days."

"Sleep?" King said. "Why it's the middle of the night."

"Exactly," I said.

"Exactly!" King said. "So let's go out and find us some nice fresh garbage."

"Oh," I said.

And we left.

CHAPTER 10

On the Streets

"You sick or something?" King asked.

I had been sniffling ever since we left the basement, and now I had a runny nose and was sneezing too. "I think I'm getting a cold," I said. "I never realized how much my tail fur helped keep me warm."

"They say ninety percent of your body heat escapes through your tail," Amelia said.

"So Harold," King said. "Since this is your first night of scavenging, we're gonna start you off with the good stuff:

restaurant trash. Where should we go, Amelia?"

"Well, that's always the question in New York, isn't it? So many choices." She stopped walking to think. "We did Chinese last night, and it seems like we do Italian every night. . . . You know what? I'd love some falafel. Let's go to that place on Broadway—Jerusalem. They must have put out the trash by now."

King and Amelia knew how to keep out of sight. We traveled through alleys, along the edges of buildings, beneath iron railings, in street gutters hugging the curb, and under parked cars. Turning the corner onto Broadway, King stuck his nose up in the air and followed the trail of an aroma I didn't find the least bit appetizing. "Mm-mm-mm! Smell that Jerusalem! Best falafel in the city."

Jerusalem Restaurant occupied a small storefront with a blue awning. Across the front, the menu was painted against a background of palm trees, a list of foods—shawarma, tabouleh, shish taouk—that I had never heard of. Piled against the lamppost near the street were three bags of trash.

King smelled each of the bags in turn. He returned to the second one and sniffed it all over. He settled on one area and took a long whiff. "That's the spot!" He started slashing away at the bag with his claws.

"Can he *do* that?" I whispered to Amelia. "I mean, it must be against the law."

"A rat does what a rat must do," she said.

For all his fury, the hole King made in the bag was a small one. He grabbed a tattered flap of the opening in his teeth and pulled, creating a much bigger hole. Out tumbled a half dozen little brownish-black balls. King knocked a couple toward me with his tail. "Here, have some."

"Is it food?" I asked.

"Of course it's food, what do you think? This is falafel," he said. He took a bite out of it and showed me. The falafel was green on the inside, like a pistachio.

I gave mine a poke, gently, as if it were likely to explode. "Is it a kind of nut?"

"No, it's Middle Eastern food," Amelia said between bites. "It's made of chickpeas and garlic and parsley and spices. Try it, it's delicious."

I remained suspicious. The little dark crusty ball sure didn't smell like food. It made me sneeze. I nibbled off a tiny bit, but it tasted awful so I only pretended to swallow it, hungry though I was. "Mmm, ith good," I lied, the falafel still in my mouth. When neither King nor Amelia were looking, I spit it out.

Someone turned the corner onto Broadway. My heart began to pump. "People are coming! People are coming!" I said. "Let's go! Let's hide!"

"Ah, forget about them," King said. "This is New

59

York—we mind our business, they'll mind theirs."

The man passed us by with only a glance. "I don't get it," I said. "The other day in the park I was chased away, and then walking down the street there was a girl who started screaming."

"There are rules," King said. "People don't like to see rats during the day. They don't like to see rats in buildings or parks. And they don't like to see rats *moving*. They're afraid we're coming for them. To do what, I don't know."

We headed back up Broadway. King and Amelia were talking about how delicious the falafel was, and it was making me hungrier and hungrier. I asked, "Do either of you know any garbage cans where we might locate some nuts? Perhaps there's a nut store around?"

Amelia smiled and King laughed. "Harold my friend, there's no menu when you're a rat. Everything's a Special of the Day."

I didn't want to look stupid, so I said, "It's just that in the park, there are nuts everywhere you look. They're very high in protein, you know."

King rolled his eyes. "OK, you don't like falafel. Well, I know—" King was cut off by the *whah-whah-whah* of a garbage truck. "Hmp. Looks like the end of the night for us. We'll have to find you something tomorrow." The garbage truck wailed again. "Boy I hate that sound," King said.

Back in the basement, I followed the rats to an old greenish-blue suitcase—their nest. King lifted the top and Amelia climbed in. "After you," King said to me. When I hesitated, he asked, "What's the matter?"

"Well, it's just, I've always slept alone."

"Alone! Why that's tragic. No wonder you're so messed up. Go on," he said, and pushed me in.

"C'mon over next to me Harold," Amelia said. "Don't worry, it's quite comfortable in here."

"Comfortable?" King said. "Don't be modest, it's luxurious." To me he said, "Amelia's constantly bringing bits of cloth and stuff back to spruce up the place."

"It's lovely," I said, although I couldn't see. I lay down. Omar was already inside.

"Yep. Nothing like a full nest," King said, and squeezed in. The two of them went right to sleep, but I couldn't. Although my feet were sore and I was exhausted, it was hard to fall asleep between two rats I had just met. Plus it was morning. Morning was for frolicking in the trees, lying out in the sun, filling your belly with nuts. But at least I was in a warm, safe place, and I was no longer alone.

CHAPTER 11

Unwritten Rules

It had taken most of the day, but I had finally managed to fall asleep when King gave me a rude and rough shake. "Up and at 'em, Harold, welcome to your first full night of life as a rat!" It was not the nicest way to wake up.

After he, Amelia, and I had scaled the wall, King yelled down, "Hey Omar, we're going now." The old rat couldn't make it up the wall anymore, so he almost never left the basement. "What do you want us to bring back for you? Bread? Some fruit?"

"Squirrels meat," he said.

"Don't worry, he's kidding," King said. "He's got a wonderful sense of humor."

Changing the subject, I said, "So where are we going tonight?"

"Well, it being a Monday, we should go after the domestic trash, meaning apartment buildings and such. People eat at home on Mondays. Now, you're lucky you're with a couple of professionals here, rats who know the neighborhood, know which buildings have the quality refuse."

"Refuse?" I asked.

"It's a fancy word for trash—I know you're only a squirrel, but try to keep up." King went on, "On Broadway, you've got your big apartment buildings, twenty floors and up, with hundreds of people. Lots of good food for the taking, right?"

"Right," I said, wanting to be agreeable.

"Wrong! In the big buildings the trash is professionally wrapped, double-bagged, very hard to penetrate. They've got huge metal bins where they keep the garbage under lock and key. You'd have to be a super rat to get into one of those." King shook his head.

"So we want to go to a small building?" I said.

"Yes, the small buildings are good because the people who live in them take out their own trash, and they just put it back in whatever bag the food came in. Half the time they don't even bother tying it up."

"King, maybe we should stop lecturing and start scavenging?" Amelia said.

"All right, all right, fine. We're there, anyway." King

stopped in front of a town house with a high stoop leading up to the front door. Three metal garbage cans were chained together in a little cement yard beside the stoop. They were beat up and full of dents, and had the number 616 written on them.

"Now Harold," King said. "Why are we starting here?"

"Because it's a small building?" I said.

"Partially. But we're starting at this *particular* town house because of the address, six sixteen. Any building ending in a six is sure to have great garbage. It's an unwritten rule of the universe."

"Are there any bad numbers?" I asked.

"Zeroes. Any building ending in zero, forget about it."

"How about six ten over on a Hundred and Fourth Street?" Amelia said. "You love their garbage."

"That's the Exception," King said. "Every rule, you see, has an Exception. The Exception proves the rule."

"I don't understand," I said.

"You don't have to understand, Harold, that's why I'm telling you, so you'll just know." And with that, King scurried up the side of a can, shoved his way under the lid with a rattle, and vanished. Thirty seconds later the cover lifted, forced up by a bag that looked as if it were struggling its way to freedom. Finally the bag dropped and the lid came

clanking down. I was afraid it clipped King. "Are you OK?" I called.

"Of course I'm OK," came King's voice, echoing inside the can. A moment later another bag came wiggling out, and King was on to the next can.

The first bag was loosely tied by the handles. Amelia grabbed one of them in her teeth and easily drew the knot open, spilling out a small pile of trash with an obnoxious odor. There was paper and Q-tips and black sludge. Amelia looked it over as if she were reading a newspaper. "Nothing," she declared, and moved on to the next bag.

I stared at it myself, and asked, "What's this muddy black stuff?"

"Coffee grounds."

Coffee! Finally my chance to try coffee. It didn't smell as good as when it was steaming out of a cup, but I was so hungry and curious I dipped a finger in and took a taste.

I gagged, then coughed. Bitter!

After he had forced out half a dozen bags, King poked his head out of the last can and said, "How'd we do?"

"No food," Amelia said. "But I found this lovely fabric for the nest."

"You know, the best thing for lining a nest is shredded bark," I said. "I always keep a fresh layer in mine."

"I'll have to try that," Amelia said.

"Oh, brother," King said. "I'm gonna go find something to eat."

We wound up at a small apartment building. It had a small fenced area full of overflowing trash cans. King climbed up one. "Here we go: yakisoba!" he said, and knocked a small white carton splat onto the cement. Brown noodles oozed out like worms. "And everybody loves: pizza!" King tipped a flat white cardboard box to the ground. A couple of crusts bounced up and out. I tried biting into one, but it was as hard as the sidewalk.

King was disgusted that I didn't like any of it. "You sure are fussy for a rodent."

"Sorry," I said and, embarrassed, walked through the bars of the fence. There was a sound coming from up the street, getting louder, the sound of something scraping the sidewalk.

Bark bark bark bark!

It was a dog without a leash, racing full speed—straight for me! "Oh no!" I yelled. "Loose dog! Help!"

Amelia reached through the iron fence and dragged me back to safety.

Bark bark bark bark!

The dog meant to run through the bars but smashed into them instead. He tried to angle his head so it could fit in, but all he could get through were his jaws. He snapped and gnashed his teeth and barked.

King stood on his hind legs. "Ah, get lost, you big jerk," he said. "There are leash laws in this city!"

A bald man came running down the street, a grin across his face. He pulled the dog's snout out from between the bars and snapped a leash on him. "What a good boy, chasing those bad rats," he said, like it was a baby he was talking to. "*Wooby wooby wooby*! That's my good Wally boy. Yes it is! You're gonna get those rats!" Man and dog walked away, both pleased with themselves.

King was in a rage. "People! Can't they control their stupid pets and leave us alone? I wish they'd all just go away!"

"And then what would we do for food?" Amelia asked. "Have you ever heard of rats out in the wild?"

"Have you ever heard of a city without rats?" King said. "Wherever there are people, there are rats and vice versa. Rats and people," he said to me, "live in what they call a 'sympathetic relationship.' What people like to eat, we like to eat. People like to fill up their houses with stuff, and so do we."

"Why do people hate rats so much anyway?" I asked, then remembered I did too, once.

"It wasn't always that way," King said. "Back in Roman times, rats were worshiped by people. We were treated like gods and it was the cats who were hated and hunted." A look of happiness came to King's face. "Those must've been the days!"

"What happened?"

"The Black Plague happened. A plague, y'see, is a kind of disease," King said. "It spreads real fast and kills lots of people. The Black Plague killed half of everybody. This was, like, a thousand years ago. Anyway, somebody figured out that people were catching the plague from rats, and we've had to watch our backs ever since."

"Well, was it true?" I asked. "About rats spreading the plague?"

"Sure it was true! Rats and people are nearly the same genetically as well as mentally. You can look it up. That's why scientists experiment on rats to find out what happens to people. You haven't ever heard of squirrels getting experimented on, have you?"

"No. I haven't."

"I didn't think so," King said proudly.

CHAPTER 12
Beautiful Places

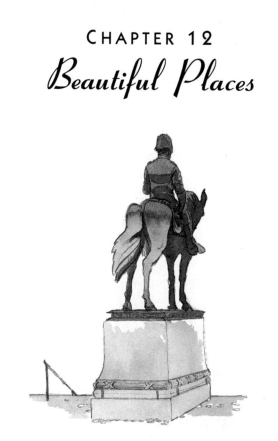

"Ah-*choo!*"

"Gesundheit!"

"Ah-*choo!*"

"Gesundheit!"

"Ahhhh-*choo!*"

"Oh *stop* it already! Some of us are trying to get some sleep over here," King hollered, and rolled away from me. I felt like sneezing more but I wrinkled my nose and sniffed and managed to stifle it.

We had just returned from a night out. I had forced

myself to eat some uncooked spaghetti, a couple o
strands that had been thrown away with the box. The
didn't taste like much, but I like hard food and at leas
they weren't moldy or dirty or smelly.

King was asleep. I gently crawled over him and exite
the suitcase. I sat on the dirt floor and stared at the hole
watching it get light out. I had been with the rats almos
a week. Would I ever adjust to this new life?

"Don't you ever sleep?" Amelia was awake too.

"Oh, sure, it just takes me some time," I said. "Did
wake you?"

"Don't worry, I'm a bit of a morning rodent myself,
Amelia said, and went to climb the wall. "Come on out
side, Harold. I want to show you something."

We went down the block to the mansion on the cor
ner. We climbed up a drainpipe and along the gutter t
the front of the roof. We were high up, overlookin
Riverside Park—I got a shiver just thinking about th
place.

"I love that man on the horse over there," she saic
pointing down.

"There's a statue just like it in Straus Park," I saic
"Made of bronze, I mean."

"I know," Amelia said. "You've told me."

"Oh, I did?" I said, embarrassed. "Yeah, I guess I dic
I guess I talk too much about the park. I promise myse
I'll stop but then I get reminded of it and I have to sa
something."

"It's OK," she said. "You're homesick."

"Even Omar told me to shut up about it the other day. 'd forgotten he could even speak. I mean, I know it's only a raffic island, but it was mine, and everything was so beau- iful there."

"Look at the river flowing by, how the color of the water natches the sky. And the boats. Things are beautiful here oo, Harold," Amelia said. "A lot of life is just getting used o things. Like food. You really have to eat more—you're 'un down. That's why your cold won't go away."

Reminded, I coughed a few times. "I guess you'r
right," I said, but I hoped she wasn't, because I didn't wan
to get used to this being a rat. That reminded me to look a
my tail. Still bald. I wondered if maybe there was some
thing vital in the hair of a squirrel's tail that he can't liv
without. Maybe it wasn't a cold I had—maybe I was dying
from lack of tail fur.

"Do you see that long, flat boat Harold?" Amelia said
pointing at the river. "That's a trash barge. Can you imag
ine? A whole floating city of trash! We'd never have t
sneak through garbage cans or rip open plastic bags if w
lived on one of those."

That didn't sound very nice to me, but I pretended she
was talking about my island and said, "Yes, Amelia, i
sounds magical." Across the river there was a gray strip o
land covered with buildings. "What's that over there?" I
asked.

"That, my dear Harold," Amelia said, "is a very won
derful place called 'New Jersey.'"

I felt a shiver. "I had no idea it was so close!"

CHAPTER 13

Rat Philosophy

"Reading lumps is an art, you know. You gotta use smell, touch, sight, even hearing," King said, pressing an ear against a garbage bag, one in a pile of many. "I can *hear* that this is office stuff inside, papers and such. Not worth the effort." He walked to the next bag. "This one's a Hefty—very popular brand in the kitchen. And this bulge here," he pointed at a round lump, "is obviously a piece of fruit of some sort. Watch," he said, and went to work. It wound up, however, being a burned-out lightbulb.

"Let's just open all the bags," Amelia said. "Harold, you take that freshly put out one." She pointed to a bag that sat off by itself, with a shape like the fat stomach of a man seated on a park bench. Steam rose off the plastic like breath.

"I'm not sure I'm qualified," I said. I had never committed a crime before.

"Don't be such a wimp," King called.

The plastic felt like skin, and was warm to the touch. I pushed where there was a bulge, and I half expected the bag to say something, to go *Ouch!* or moan or say *Get away from me!*

"I'm sorry about this," I said to the bag, and pressed in with my claws until they poked through. I pulled away but the bag kept stretching. Finally it broke off and snapped back, leaving a little patch of plastic between my claws. I tried to shake it off, but I had to use my teeth. The bag showed only a minute puncture wound.

"Over here, Harold!" Amelia called. "I found some bones!"

I was saved.

There wasn't much meat on the bones, and I had no idea from what animal they had come, but I gnawed on one like I saw King and Amelia do. The flavor wasn't bad.

As usual, King talked about his theories and I thought about my park. Were there any leaves left on the trees? Had the man with the walker gone to Florida yet? Did anyone wonder what happened to me? "I bet Sidney ate good today," I said. "On Tuesdays the lady with the Brazil nuts comes."

"What's the adventure in that?" King said. "When you're a rat, there are no regular feeding times. Life isn't planned, it *happens*." He chewed on his bone for a bit. "Take that little trouble we had with the dog the other night—stuff like that happens all the time. A rat always has to be on the alert."

King made the life sound romantic, but when you thought about it, it just seemed difficult.

The next building had two black trash cans and two blue ones. King managed to tip over one of the blue ones, and there was such a terrible clanking of glass bottles that I was sure half the block would wake up. Bottles rolled over the sidewalk, a couple making it onto the street. "I think maybe we shouldn't knock over the blue cans," I said. "It looks like these people sorted their recycling very carefully."

"Oh, lighten up," King said.

"Well, it's just that at the park people are very careful to—"

"Oh, enough about your park!" King said. "You're the only one who ever got marooned by leaving an

75

island and joining the rest of the world!"

"Don't listen to him Harold," Amelia said. "You're absolutely right. King knows perfectly well there's never anything but empty bottles in those blue containers. He just likes to make a big noise."

"Ah that's a bunch of——" and King said a word that I can't repeat here.

I didn't feel like going through any more garbage, or listening to any more of King's theories. I turned to walk away but stopped short. I was face-to-face with an unfamiliar rat. He was hunched down, his tail flat against the ground, and his coat was grimy, nearly black. A common rat.

Then I realized—I was looking in a mirror someone had put out with the trash.

CHAPTER 14

A Good Dream

I was in my park dancing from branch to branch along the treetops. It was as if my feet weren't even touching the branches, and then indeed they weren't, and I was flying. I had glorious white wings on my back, like Terrence's, and my full, bushy tail trailed behind me in the breeze. I flew around the tall apartment buildings and saw the people living one on top of the other. Through one of the windows I saw Macadamia. His apartment was filled with nothing but piles and piles of nuts.

I flew higher, above the water towers. How funny Strau
Park looked from up here, a little green island in the gra
concrete sea of New York. I flew over Riverside Park and it
hundreds of squirrels and they were all pointing up, jealou
now. I flapped my wings in strong, proud strokes. Across th
Hudson River and to New Jersey I soared. It was filled wit
happy rats and pigeons, none of them hiding, none of then
fighting.

I flew down the Hudson, over the huge boats in the har
bor. There was one ten times bigger than the rest. Acros
the side of it was written *H.M.S. Titanic*, and on deck wa
an older couple holding hands. Somehow I knew it wa
Isidor and Ida Straus.

At the mouth of the harbor I circled the Statue o
Liberty, the torch flaming real fire. I could see all of Nev
York, from the Battery up to the Bronx, the buildings an
bridges and islands big and small that Terrence had tol
me about. I flew higher and higher until New York was
little dot, and the sun enormous. Everything went white
and a moment later I was above the clouds, drenched i
golden sunlight. This must be heaven, I thought. I ha
flown so high I had made it to heaven.

Then I woke up and I was in a dark, dank basemen
curled up inside a suitcase with three rats. It had been
dream. But it was so *real*. I checked my back, expectin
there to be wings, but no, just a skinny tail, as hairless a
could be.

Why can't it be true? I thought. Why can't I have wing
and fly away from all this? There are flying squirrels, aren

there? I've never seen any, but I know they exist.

I pressed my eyelids shut and tried to return to the dream. I flapped my wings, I remembered the sensation of flying, but the dream wouldn't take, and I found myself thinking, maybe it wasn't just the wings I dreamed up. Maybe I had dreamed my entire life as a squirrel, and really, I had always been a rat. The only proof I had were my memories, which were no better than dreams.

"C'mon, you lazy treehopper. Get off your keister— time to go to work."

It was King.

I couldn't bear another night of hunting for trash. I just wanted to stay curled up in the suitcase and feel sorry for myself. "No thank you," I said.

"C'mon," King said, and yanked me on the tail.

"Please go," I said. "I don't feel well." I coughed weakly.

Amelia leaned down to my ear. "Is everything okay?" she whispered.

I wanted to throw my arms around her and cry, but I buried my head deeper in my arms and said, "I'm just not hungry is all."

"Ah, let him starve," King said.

CHAPTER 15
The Apple Core Incident

I was glad when King and Amelia left. For a little while, anyway. Then I got hungry. Very hungry. I couldn't stop thinking about food, about how much I wanted food—any kind of food. Food, food, food! What I wouldn't have given for some falafel, a petrified bit of orange peel, a crumb of rock-hard bread—anything that at any time had ever been considered food.

"Omar?" I said.

"Rrrr," he grumbled.

"Omar," I said, "you wouldn't have any food stashed away would you? A little bit of hamburger or something? A piecrust maybe?"

"Rrrr," he grumbled again. "Still sleeping—no foods—go away!"

I picked myself up and went to find King and Amelia. I checked the usual spots, the restaurants, all the buildings ending in six, but no luck.

What to do? I had never rooted through garbage alone before, but I was *so hungry*.

I was on 108th, a good street. I walked up and down the block looking for the right opportunity. I didn't want to climb into a garbage can; that was too scary to attempt alone. What if the lid came back down on top of me and I got trapped inside?

The door to one of the town houses opened. A man dragged a bag of trash down the steps and deposited it on the sidewalk under a wispy ginkgo tree. After he had gone back inside, I walked past the bag once, then back the other way, and finally went up to it. The bag was full to bursting, and I sniffed it all over, like I had seen King do.

Oh! Something smelled delicious inside! What was it? I pressed my nose against the bag and breathed in deeply.

Mmmmmmm. Apples. Probably spotty, mealy apples, but I'd have given anything for just the taste of one.

The black plastic bulged where it smelled the most apple-y. I looked around to make sure no one was watching. I found the courage, sunk a claw into the plastic, tugged a bit, and made a small tear in the bag. The smell of apple exploded into the night air and I found myself digging at the bag with a fury I didn't know I had. Suddenly, the bag *burst* open and I was drowning in garbage.

The apple core was one of the last things to spill out. It was a big juicy one, not just seeds and stem but one with lots of meat and red skin still on the top and bottom. It rolled onto the sidewalk and down the hill toward Riverside. I pounced on it just as it was picking up speed. I spent one last moment savoring the smell, then I dug in.

It was delicious—the most delicious thing I had ever eaten! It wasn't even mealy, and barely yellowed. I took small bites so I would have longer to enjoy it. What a feast!

The only two things in the world were me and that apple. Then, there was another thing, a sound, a sound I had heard before, the sound of twenty scraping toenails. I looked up. There was a dog coming at me full speed. *The dog*—the leashless dog!

He was practically on top of me, his mouth open, ready to strike. The sensible thing would have been to flee immediately—but my apple core! That apple core was my best friend in the whole world at the moment and I couldn't leave him behind. I picked it up like an ear of corn, bit in, and leapt away. There was a metal railing that ran in front of the town houses. I did a corkscrew spiral up the nearest post, and as I did, the dog was upon me.

I could feel his hot breath on my bare tail, could smell that night's dog food. He leapt up, but I was already racing down the rail. He followed me, half a breath behind. I was an inch above his head, hurdling every post, leaping across stoops, the apple core still clenched in my mouth. He could reach up and grab me if he gained even one step, and that was about to become unavoidable: I was running out of rail!

I stopped on a dime and reversed direction. I chanced a look back and saw the dog still running along the rail the other way, thinking he was in hot pursuit. He slowed to a trot, finally suspecting something. He stopped at the end of the railing, looked up, down, and all around, with a bewildered expression on his face.

I hopped down to the sidewalk, raced up the ginkgo tree under which I had found the trash bag, and resumed my dinner. The dog wandered back up the hill to the spot

where he had found me, right underneath the branch I was perched on. He poked his rapidly sniffing nose into the bag where I had torn the hole, picked up a scent, and followed it in.

Running down the street came the bald man holding a leash bunched in his fist. "Wa-Wa-Wallace Alexander!" he panted. "That's whe-whe-where you've been!" The dog lifted his head up, but it was stuck in the bag. He started to shake and thrash wildly, throwing trash everywhere. Finally, the man pulled the bag off the dog's head, yanked him up by the collar, and snapped the leash on. "Ho-ho-honestly Wally, tearing open garbage bags! No more off the leash time for you!"

I ate every last bit of my apple core. As I sat in the tree
sucking on the stem, I thought about the two things I had
learned that night. One, dogs are stupid. Two, rooting
through garbage can be the most satisfying thing in the
world.

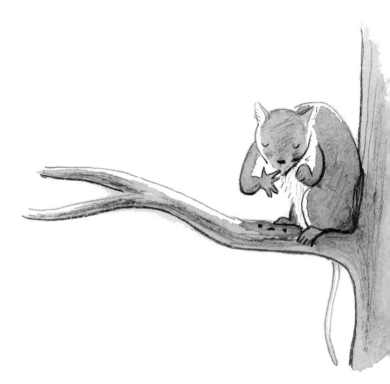

CHAPTER 16

Glutton

I would never become as bold or courageous as King, but I began to do my part when it came to finding food. I realized that people do throw away a lot of perfectly good food, and that the difference between food and garbage is largely a matter of opinion. Lots of things were better. I was getting used to sleeping during the day. I had gotten over my cold. But I was still homesick for my island.

"Why don't you go for a visit?" Amelia said to me one night.

"I told you how I had to leave," I said.

"But that was before you knew how to get around as a rat," she said.

"I'm not sure . . ."

"Go now! The sun's nearly up. It's your favorite time of day, isn't it?"

So it was almost against my will that I found myself walking to Straus Park. My heart was filled with both excitement and dread.

The park was gray and empty. All the leaves had fallen from the trees, and no people were around. It seemed impossibly small. Surely, .44 acres was bigger than this? It took one minute to walk from the sign at the entrance to the statue of Memory. It used to be the furthest distance I would walk in a day, and now it was, well, nowhere.

I gazed for a moment into the downcast eyes of Memory, and at least she was exactly as I had pictured her.

"Ay! Baldy!" came a voice out of the statue. "You! Yeah you! Good to see you back here."

I went behind the statue of Memory and found Sidney. He was lying on his back, his stomach as high as his body was long. His arms and legs were like toothpicks sticking out of a Thanksgiving turkey. The very thought of Sidney had  always made me angry, but now he looked too ridiculous to be mad at.

"I was just getting ready to go to sleep," he said.

"Why aren't you sleeping up in the nest?" I asked.

"'Cause I'm too *fat*," Sidney said, and patted the sides of
his stomach. "Ain't it great? I got the girth of a sumo
wrestler. All these nuts—fattening y'know. I can't believe
you used to bury the stuff. You must have self-control or
something. Not me, I'm a glutton."

I wasn't sure what glutton meant, but my guess was
"dangerously overweight rat."

"Not that it was just the nuts. There was this street festi-
val—oh, squirrel boy, you should've seen it—people just
throwing food at me from every direction. There was Greek
souvlaki, pad thai, Mexican roasted corn, Italian sausage,
French crêpes—I
went around the
world and I never
left Broadway. I passed
out, I ate so much."

"So how long have you
been there on your back?" I
asked.

"Not sure. A couple days, maybe five."

"Can you get up?"

"I dunno, I haven't tried. But I can sure do this: whee,
whee, whee!" he said, and rocked from one side to the other,
like he was a boat in a stormy sea. "Whee, whee, whee!"

"That's very impressive," I said.

"Thanks. And flouncy, I owe it all to you. You, and this
magnificent tail," he said, and flicked it. As he did, a couple
of hairs flew loose and danced in the air a moment before

coming to rest on the ground. There were big chunks of tail fur missing. In fact, the entire underside was pretty much bare.

"Well, I should be going," I said, depressed by how Sidney was living my former life. "I'll tell King and the others that you said hello."

"King! And Amelia and Omar! You friends with them? Wait a minute, don't leave. Here, I'll get up," he said. He began rocking again. Instead of side to side, he went forward and back like he was struggling to get a grip on an imaginary rope.

With a loud "Uh!" he made one great lunge forward. He was pulling with his neck, making gurgling sounds under the strain. Just as his eyes looked ready to pop out of his head, his head snapped back against the pavement and knocked him out. A flurry of my old tail hair was released into the air and carried away on a breeze.

After checking to make sure he was still breathing, I left Sidney lying there, his tongue hanging out of his mouth, a big fat mound of rat.

CHAPTER 17

Big Time at Black Rock

I had been hearing about it every night for weeks. It was going to be a "big time," King said. Thanksgiving—the first party of the season at Black Rock. Every rat who was any rat would be there.

"The holiday season is the best time to be a rat," King said, lying next to me Thanksgiving morning. "From tonight through Christmas right up to New Year's Day the trash bins are stuffed with turkey and ham and bread and cake. A rat doesn't hardly have to work. Whenever he's hungry, he just goes to the nearest garbage can and get something delicious."

Without so much work, rats had more time to socialize and the best place in New York to socialize was Black Rock. "You've never been uptown Harold, so you don't know. Once you cross 110th Street, everything changes. It's where the university is."

"University?"

"It's where people go to learn," King said. "Or they're supposed to anyway. Mostly they throw a lot of good food away. Four in the morning, they'll toss a half-eaten slice of pizza on the ground. It's fantastic."

"So why don't we move uptown?" I asked.

"The competition! There's tons of food, but you have to fight three other rats for every scrap." Like being a pigeon, I thought. "Uptown, it can be tough just finding a place to sleep." King shook his head at the trouble. "Black Rock is on a Hundred and Fourteenth Street, the most rat-infested block in Manhattan. It said so right in the *New York Times* and they print all the news that fits, so it must be true."

"What's it like?" I asked. "Black Rock."

"Oh, it's too incredible to describe," King said. A look of wonder came to his face. "It's a place where only rats are allowed. If your island is a squirrel's paradise, well, Black Rock is a rat's."

King drifted off to sleep, but I was too excited. I had never been to a party before. I watched the light from the window move across the floor as the sun passed over Manhattan, dust flickering brilliantly in its path. It slowly walked up the staircase, step by step, turning yellow, gold, orange, fading all the while, and as it was about to reach the door, it burned out.

I shook King awake. "It's sundown, let's go. Are you ready?" I said.

King rolled onto his back, yawned, and stretched. "We'll go in an hour or so," he said.

"But you said the party started when it got dark."

"Yeah, yeah, it does, but in New York you never want to be on time to a party." He wrinkled his nose. "It's rude. You have to be at least an hour late. Two is better."

That didn't sound right, so I woke up Amelia. "Oh yes, it's very rude to show up on time to a party," she said. I was disappointed that I had to wait, but I didn't want to be rude.

We finally left, but the trip lasted forever because of Omar. It took all three of us to shove him up the wall, and then he walked slowly and kept bumping into things.

The air was fresh and smelled of firewood burning and you could even see a star or two, a rare thing in New York. We traveled up Riverside Drive and turned at 114th Street. I was nervous. I was about to meet hundreds of rats.

The hill up from Riverside was much steeper here. We had climbed almost to Broadway and I didn't see anything that looked like a big black rock. Could it be much smaller than I was expecting? There was just a row of town houses and a big apartment building on the corner.

And then, there it was.

Between the buildings, behind a tall iron fence was a rock bigger than any I could have imagined. It reached up over two stories and was so black it seemed to absorb the light of the street lamps. The surface stabbed out in all directions. Discarded old cans, bottles, coffee cups, flyers, and delivery menus had collected in the crevices. Scrub trees clung precariously to the rock and swayed in the breeze. Black Rock stood horrible and desolate. It was the exact opposite of my golden island.

"Ain't it great!" King said enthusiastically.

Black Rock looked unscalable, but between the jagged outcroppings were pathways that led from the street to the summit.

I kept slipping because it was hard to find footing. As we wound our way up, I started to hear the murmur of voices, and then, at the very top, everything came into view.

I felt uneasy, a little sick. There were whole turkeys and chickens scattered about, cans of every kind of soup and vegetable and gravy imaginable, plus pizzas, potato chips, Jell-O, french fries, cupcakes—everything. And all around, rats. Hundreds of them, laughing, joking, and eating. King, Amelia, and Omar were immediately swallowed up by the crowd. Everyone was their best friend.

Someone bumped into me and said, "Excuse me, friend,

didn't see you back there." He turned to face me, a small
at with a nice white smile. Then he looked me over and the
orners of his mouth turned down. "You're not from
round here, are you? Are you from the Bronx or some-
ing? Westchester?" He squinted suspiciously. "You have
n exotic look to you."

"Actually, I'm a squirrel. My name's Harold."

The rat's eyes bobbled in his head with surprise, and he
urst into laughter. "Huh-huh-ho! Squirrels at Black Rock!
thought I'd seen everything. Hey, Two! Three! Come over
ere! You've got to meet this one!"

Two rats identical to my new acquaintance came over t
where we were standing. "Harold, I want you to meet m
brothers, Two and Three. My name's One-Nine."

"We were all in the same litter," Two said with the sam
great smile. "Our mom named us after the subway train
We were born in the Ninety-Sixth Street station."

"Under the express tracks," Three added with prid
"Where are you from?"

I told them my story and they started laughing, and
found myself laughing too. It suddenly seemed funny,
squirrel who looked like a rat. Two, Three, and One-Nin
kept inviting their friends over, and I felt like a celebrit
Every time I told the story I made it longer and funnie
and I even added some things that were not strictly true.

"Hey, this guy's all right for a squirrel," someone said

"Boy, I would've never pegged him for a treehopper
said another. "No one would."

"Hey, you know who Harold has to meet," One-Nir
said. "The Professor!"

"The Professor! Yes! Right!" everyone agreed.

"Who's the Professor?" I asked One-Nine as we mac
our way through the party.

"You've never heard of the Professor?" One-Nine sai
shocked. "Why, he's a legend! Black Rock is *his* rock! He
lived here longer than anyone can remember. Before th
he was a lab rat up at the university. The scientists we
doing super top-secret research on him, but he was to
intelligent for them. He's the only one ever to escape."

"You should hear his stories." Two shook off a chi

Endless mazes and running in wheels. The things they made him do!"

One-Nine led me to a high plateau. An audience gathered below. Out of the crowd came an elegant snow-white rat with a long body and blinking pink eyes. Two and Three escorted him up to the plateau; then the three brothers left the Professor and me alone on what now seemed a stage.

"Hello," I said, "I'm—"

"Zilence!" The Professor stopped me. He was looking me over from head to tail with one eye squinting and one wide open.

"So what kind of a rat you make him out to be, Professor?" someone hollered.

"Hmp! He'z a very interezting zpezimen," the Professor said. "Zomeone get me my magnifying glazz zo I can make a clozer inzpection."

Someone handed up a broken pair of eyeglasses. Both arms were missing and so was one of the lenses. The Professor held them up by the broken frame and investigated me with the intact lens and a lot of poking. "M-hm, m-hm," he said. "Egzellent muzzle tone. Very broad zhoulderz." He came

around to my front and grabbed my top lip, pulling it up t
my nose to study my teeth. "A-ha, yez, definitely *rodenti*
but obviouzly not *Rattuz norvegica*." He grabbed one of m
front legs and yanked it out to the side, then began closel
investigating my claws. "Not *Rattuz rattuz*, either."

"Give it up, Professor!" King yelled. "You'll never fig
ure it out!"

But the Professor ignored King as he walked aroun
the back of me, grabbed the tip of my tail, and ran his eye
glass back and forth over it. "M-hm, m-hm." Suddenly, h
thrust his fist with my tail still in it straight up in the a
"Here iz the evidenze, exactly as I zuzpected it to be!" th
Professor announced triumphantly "Notize, if you will, th
lack of zcalez on the tail, common to every order of rat
Notize alzo, pleaze, ztubble!" There were oohs and al
from the crowd. "The telltale zignz of returning ha
growth! Becauze thiz iz not a rat at all, but an egzample o
Zciuruz carolinenziz, otherwize known az the commo
gray zquirrel!"

The crowd began to cheer and
there were yells of *Bravo!*
I couldn't help but
smile.

*   *   *

"And then did you see how everybody cheered?"

"Yes, yes, we saw how everybody cheered."

"And then the way Professor and I got carried around on everyone's backs?"

"We saw it all, Harold."

"Everyone sure was nice," I said. "And to find out my tail hair is finally growing back too!"

We were back in the suitcase, but I was still light-headed from the excitement. "Y'know, I don't think I ever had a night that exciting in my whole life."

"I told you it was gonna be like that," King said. "It's like that every night at Black Rock. Now pipe down. I need my beauty sleep."

CHAPTER 18

Christmas in the City

December was fantastic, festive, and fun. Every night was a different party at Black Rock, and we went to all of them. Some were theme parties, like who could bring the biggest bone. King and I spent hours going through garbage cans until we found a T-bone so tremendous that it took the two of us plus Amelia to carry it. We came in second to a turkey thighbone that looked like it came from a Tyrannosaurus rex.

One of my favorite parts of a Black Rock evening was

the walk there. New York was in such good cheer during the holidays that nobody cared about a few harmless rats wandering the streets. We could stroll up Broadway right out in the open. At Straus Park, there had never been any Christmas decorations, but above 110th Street they were everywhere. Santa Claus and reindeer flew across every store window, small forests of fresh-cut trees stood for sale on the sidewalks, and every corner had a man selling freshly roasted chestnuts. Oh, the smell of them!

One night I saw a man buy a brown paper bag full of chestnuts from a vendor. "I've never tried them before," he said as he paid. King, Amelia, Omar, and I followed him, and my mouth watered in jealousy as he drew one from the bag. He examined it curiously for a moment, then nibbled off a piece. He stopped walking, spit it out, said "Uck!" and tossed the still full bag right onto the street. Amelia and I dragged the bag under a car and we dug in. They were the first nuts I had eaten since I left the park, and they were rich and buttery and smoky and delicious.

At Christmas we exchanged presents—King gave me a "tail mitten," meaning an old sock. We all laughed. My tail had grown out enough that you could see the stubble, even without a magnifying glass. It was thrilling, but itchy.

New Year's Eve was the biggest party yet. Rats came from as far away as Harlem and the Upper East Side to go to it. One had even caught the subway up from Times Square. The Professor had a beautiful old pocket watch with a cracked face, and we all gathered around it to count down to midnight and cheer in the New Year.

Freezing though it was, our good feelings made the trip home easy—until we reached our corner. We were met there by a bitter cold wind that was blowing up the street off the Hudson River. It was whipping so hard it pushed us back a step. We huddled close together and leaned our way into the wind down the hill.

"There's nothing I hate," King said, "like winter."

CHAPTER 19

A Woeful Tale

It was as if the streets had grown old and died. There were no more parties at Black Rock, no more decorations, and the green Christmas trees that had lined Broadway, bursting with good smells and the promise of presents, were out on the sidewalks with the rest of the trash, brittle skeletons lying in pale brown puddles of their own fallen needles.

In my cozy nest protected from the wind, I'd always slept away most of the winter, coming down only to take my meals. A rat's winter is entirely different. The basement was warm, but at night our paws froze on the icy sidewalks. Even decent garbage was getting harder to come by. People seemed to have stopped throwing good food away, and if it snowed it was nearly impossible to dig the trash bags out anyway.

"The worst thing about January," King said, "is that you know February will be even worse."

And so it was. It snowed almost every day that month. We were coming home empty-handed so often that Amelia, King, and I began to split up so we could cover more ground.

One night I was assigned a stretch of Broadway just north of Straus Park. Outside of a Cuban restaurant I found a bag with some promising lumps. It was a particularly tough bag, a thick double-ply number. I was scratching away when, without warning, I felt two arms reach around my stomach from behind and lock me in a bear hug. I tried to break away, but the grip was too tight.

"You've got to *help me*!" a voice behind me wailed. "Please!"

"Let me go!" I yelled, terrified.

"*Help me help me help me!*"

I finally broke my assailant's grip and turned around to see a familiar face. It was even skinnier and more desperate than when I had seen it for the first time, months before. "Man alive, Sidney! What's wrong with you?"

"*This* is what's wrong with me!" he wailed, and pulled around his tail. My fur was gone, and in its place were stubby little brown things. What they were, I had no idea.

"After the last of the tail fur fell off, everyone aban-
doned me! No one loves me anymore!" Sidney sobbed. "The
ingratitude! The way I used to dance and flick my tail for
them! Then I go bald and everyone drops me like a bad
habit. Oh, that Macadamia," Sidney said, wagging a claw at
me, anger replacing tears. "He was the first to turn. As soon
as the tail started thinning out he stopped with the good
nuts. Forget the macadamias, a peanut or two *maybe*, and
then, nothing!"

"I don't know what I can—"

"And the old guy! You know, the *really* old guy? With
the pistachios and the walker? He stopped coming to the
park altogether." Sidney looked around nervously and
whispered in my ear, his voice cracking with emotion, "I
fear the worst." He sniffled and his eyes narrowed to teary
slits. "I think maybe he's dead."

"Oh, I don't think so," I said, trying to comfort him.
"He goes to Florida every winter."

"What does that mean, Florida?" Sidney asked frantically. "Is Florida like heaven? Maybe it's like heaven, and he really is dead."

"No, Florida's not like heaven at all," I said. Then I thought for a minute. "Well, maybe it's on the way. . . ."

"Look, man, *forget* Florida—I'm starving over here!" Sidney grabbed me by the fur of my chest. "You gotta help me!"

"This is the most disgusting display I have ever had the misfortune to witness," said a voice from the darkness. It was  King, walking toward us, with Amelia not far behind. "Being a rat just wasn't good enough for you, huh Sidney? Now you come crawling back." King shook his head from side to side. "And after all the garbage cans we knocked over together."

Sidney couldn't look any of us in the eye. He just slouched and began to nervously pick the short brown spikes from his tail. "I'm sorry guys," he mumbled.

"What did you do to your tail?" Amelia asked.

"Oh," Sidney said, and stopped picking at it. "Well, after Harold's hair fell off, I couldn't think of anything else, so I glued some pine needles from an old Christmas tree to my tail." He shrugged. "It didn't really fool anybody." Sidney looked up and smiled sheepishly.

King shook his head again, this time more sad than
ngry. "Well," he said with a sigh, "Amelia and I had just
>me over to tell Harold we found some food. It's nothing
reat, just a stale cupcake, and I don't know why we
iould help you, but I suppose—"

"Oh thank you thank you thank you," Sidney cried,
irowing his arms around King.

And that's how Sidney came back to live with us.

CHAPTER 20
The Blizzard

It was March when the blizzard hit. The cars lining the streets, the fire hydrants, the front stoops—all of them became gentle bumps beneath the same thick white blanket. There was no way we could move through it, and we were too hungry to sleep, so we sat on the window ledge and watched. Eventually, the snow covered up our hole and we couldn't see anything until the next morning when the sidewalk got shoveled. But all there was to see was more snow.

"It's beautiful," Amelia said.

"Beautiful?" Sidney said. "Are you crazy? It's ugly! Hideous! It's the most horrible thing I've ever seen!"

"For once, I think I agree with Sidney," King said. The snow soon covered over our window again.

When we heard the scraping of the shovel the next morning, we all reluctantly climbed up the wall to go look. Even Amelia had begun to give up hope. But with a loud scrape of the cement the snow in front of our window was swept away, and sunlight burst through. It had stopped snowing, and it was warm.

We watched as the blanket of snow began to melt away. Everywhere was water dripping—it came down like rain in front of our window. The sidewalks were one long puddle, and the streets a slushy mess. There was the sound of car tires spinning, children playing, and best of all, trash can lids clinking.

"I hope no one's tired, because it's going to be a lo-o-ong night of scavenging," King said.

"There's probably a whole week's worth of garbage out here!" I said.

"We should go out now!" Sidney cried. "I'm about to pass out, I'm so starving."

"Be patient," Amelia said. "It will make it that much better later if we wait."

The sun began to go down, and it turned frigid. The water stopped dripping, and everything was still.

"That's it, I'm going," Sidney said, before it was even dark. "Make way."

"You better be careful," Amelia said. "It might be icy."

"I don't care, I got great balance," Sidney said, charging through the opening. "I'm gonna go get myself some fooooooo—"

Sidney slid past the garbage cans, through the gate across the sidewalk, and smashed headfirst into a fire hydrant, the journey recorded by a trail of scratch marks in the ice. It looked very painful.

"Sidney!" we called. "Are you OK?"

"Yeah, yeah," he said, woozy, and clawed his way back to us.

A thick layer of ice encased the entire city. Everything seemed as if it was made of glass, and it all sparkled beneath the street lamps. King and I tried to lift the lids of some garbage cans, but no luck. Each one was an enormous stout icicle, sealed shut.

We returned to our basement dejected and went back to waiting and hoping, with less hope than ever. How many days had we gone without food? Three? Four?

Sidney was the first to lose it. He had been muttering under his breath for a while, and then he exploded, hysterical: "Why are you all so calm? Are you all stupid? Don't you see we're going to starve to death? I was a fool to come back here!"

"Well at least you won't die alone," King said.

While they argued, I thought I heard something coming from outside. A voice? "Did anybody else hear that?" I asked.

"*Hello! Hello! Anybody down there?*"

We looked at each other, then turned up to face the hole and yelled, "Hello! Hello!"

A familiar head popped through the hole. "Hello?" it said.

"Two!" I yelled.

"Actually, it's One-Nine. Two is right behind me."

"Here I am." An identical face popped into view. "Hi, everybody!"

"I'm here too," said Three, jamming his head into the hole. The triplets smiled their brilliant smiles. "Word around Black Rock is that your basement is always warm and loaded with food."

"The warm part is true enough," King said, "but I'm afraid somebody lied to you about us having food."

"We're awfully cold out here," One-Nine said. "Maybe we could come down for a while?"

"Of course, of course," we said.

"We practically killed ourselves getting here. At one point I thought Two would slide all the way into the Hudson."

The three of them were fur and bones. "Things were bad uptown even before the blizzard," Two said. "There hasn't been food for a week, not since the students left on vacation. Spring break, they call it. Why doesn't anyone ever give *us* a break?"

Throughout the night our Black Rock friends came, all starving and all disappointed to learn that we were as hungry as they. Most arrived with sprains, bumps, and bruises. The Professor, who had slid headfirst into a lamppost, was still groggy, speaking nothing but Latin. "*Agricola, agricolae, agricolam . . .*"

Everyone was trying to come up with a plan. One suggestion was that we all storm the nearest restaurant, take to the tables, and eat whatever we could in the ensuing mayhem. Another was to try to find cracked-open windows and sneak into apartments to raid kitchen cabinets. None of the plans sounded good to me.

"We already have foods," Omar said, and sniffed up in the air. "Squirrels."

Everyone turned and looked at me, and I felt like a Thanksgiving turkey. I must have looked nervous, because everyone burst into laughter.

Nobody could agree on any of the plans and we were reduced to gnawing on whatever we had on hand. Cardboard, old magazines, wires—anything to hold off starvation.

"Doesn't anybody know where some

food is? Any food? Anywhere?" one of the triplets asked. It was the millionth time the question had been asked that night, and it took a million times for me to remember. To remember my former life.

"Anyone?"

"Maybe . . ." I said, and all eyes were on me. "Maybe I know where we can get some nuts."

CHAPTER 21

Buried Treasure

Hard, dirty snow had been piled up against the cars by street plows and formed craggy mountains that, while icy, offered surer footing than the sidewalks. I can't imagine what a person would have done if they had seen us, a swarm of rats out in the open, traveling along at their eye level. Thankfully, no person was foolish enough to be out on such a night.

"Now what?" Sidney said when we reached Broadway. Straus Park was in sight, its trees looking like they were

116

made of glass, twinkling in the street lamps. It looked so close, but separating it from us was a sea of ice. "Look at that street!" Sidney said. "We'll kill ourselves trying to get across."

I hadn't thought about this part.

"We'll move in a chain," King said. "Each rat takes the tail of the rat in front of him into his mouth, so that we keep each other anchored as we cross the street."

"What if a car comes? Cars are the number one killer of rats, you know," Sidney said. "Squirrels too, baldy."

"You think there's a person dumb enough to be driving on a night like tonight?" King said, and as he did, the headlights of a cab came into view, creeping up Broadway. "Ah, the Exception always proves the rule—I'm going." Everyone agreed, nervously.

After the cab had passed and we had looked in all four directions of the intersection, King ventured out onto the icy street, slipping immediately. He regained his footing and I, gently as I could, took his tail into my mouth and followed him a couple of steps. I then felt a sharp pain in my own tail—Sidney biting in. It was all I could do not to yell and let go.

The crossing seemed certain to end in disaster. Whenever one rat slipped, the entire chain would veer along with him, my stomach would drop, and Sidney would bite harder into my tail. I kept straining my eyes uptown and down, east and west, occasionally confusing a street lamp with headlights and nearly having a heart attack. But finally I made it to the curb at the entrance to the park.

"You sure about this?" King asked me, as we waited for

the rest of the rats to finish the crossing. "I mean, you remember where you buried all these nuts?"

"Sure, I'm sure," I said, although I wasn't. I had buried plenty of nuts in the park, but I had never had occasion to dig any back up. I was hoping that my squirrel instincts would take over.

We went over and stood on the flower beds, with Memory watching over us. Or rather, we stood on a crust of ice, on top of snow, on top of the ground in which flower bulbs and nuts were buried. Think, I said to myself. Twenty rats were gathered around me, anxious, hoping, skeptical. I picked a spot where I thought I remembered burying a smoked almond and began clawing at the ice, but I was literally just scratching the surface. Cold hard stares fell on me. I tried harder. My arms burned and my claws ached, but the thing was looking hopeless. What an

idiot I was, taking everyone away from our warm, safe basement, risking our lives just getting here. And for what? Nothing.

"Hey, flouncy," Sidney said, "let me give you a hand." Sidney shooed me out of the way, stood on the spot I had been marking up, and leapt high in the air. The ice cracked on impact and Sidney disappeared into the soft white powder beneath the surface. He popped back up wearing a hat of snow.

"Thanks, Sidney," I said, and hopped down. I quickly moved the snow out of the way and attacked the ground below. It was tough going, but I was making steady progress. It felt good to have fresh dirt between my claws.

I smelled the nut. Not wanting to harm my prize, I gently swept the remaining dirt away. I ran my nose all over the perfectly preserved almond. How wonderful it smelled! I drew it out with my teeth, stood on my hind legs, and held the nut victoriously up. "Here," I said, handing it to King. "Give this to the Professor."

"*Zumuz, eztiz, zunt!*" the Professor said upon hearing his name. Then King waved the almond under his nose and it shook the Professor out of his stupor. He took a bite, his pink eyes blinked wildly, and he said, "Deliciouz!"

Suddenly, everyone was grabbing at me to bring them to a spot where I had buried a nut. "Yes, right here is a good

anut, still in its shell. The Brazil nuts are over beneath
at ginkgo—no, to the left—yes, right there. Anyone who
ants cashews, follow me now. Right here, here, and here."
pointed.

I'd never felt prouder. After feeling helpless for so long,
aving to be taught everything, it felt good to show that I
new something too.

"Here Harold, try this peanut!"

"Mmm, delicious," I said.

"Over here Harold!" one of the triplets called. "Is this a
ut?" One-Nine asked with a full mouth. "It's green."

"That's a pistachio," I said.

"Wow—I *love* pistachios!"

"Oh, Harold!" Amelia said. "These macadamias are
erything you said! They are divine."

The snow, aglow under the street lamps, was dotted
ith tiny craters, and in the cold night and thin atmosphere
looked like we were searching for buried treasure on the
oon.

One by one, the rats left, bellies full and nuts in their
ouths for the journey home, the roads made safe by the
raying of salt from the city trucks. Sidney and Amelia
ok Omar back to the basement. King was the last one left
esides me. "You really saved us, Harold," he said. "It sure
as a lucky day the day you came to live with us."

"Thanks, King," I said. "Thanks for everything."

"So you ready to go?" he asked. "Sun's coming up."

"I think I'll stay here," I said. "For a little while."

King headed west, into the night. In the east the sun

121

was glowing from behind the apartment buildings, th
black of the sky above slowly giving way to blue. To get
better look I climbed the elm tree to my old nest, now
dilapidated wreck. Day coming, night going, me i
between.

Trucks came along spraying salt, and people carefull
made their way to the subways and buses. The temperatur
rose with the sun, and the ice began to melt off th
branches. The trees were weeping, and I felt that they wer
weeping tears of joy at the arrival of a new day, at th
arrival of—at long last—spring.

CHAPTER 22
Spring

"Did you smell that? That right there with the last breeze," I said. It was early morning and we were on our way home, through streets and past cars dusted light green with honey locust pollen. "Those are the azaleas."

"Ah, they stink," King said. "Now, a beautiful smell was what we found in that can on a Hundred and Ninth Street. Mexican food and banana chocolate fudge ice cream, mm-good."

"It wasn't bad," I had to admit.

"Ah, who are you kidding, Harold?" King said. "You

didn't like it half as much as you'd like a single peanut."

"That's not true," I said.

"Well, I'll tell you what *is* true Harold," King said. "It's time for you to go home to your stupid park. Your tail is back."

"No, no, I don't think it is quite yet," I said, stopping to check. For the longest time there had just been stubble, but then, all at once, it grew in. And to be honest, it was bushier now than it had ever been. "Really, I think it has quite a ways to go."

"Oh no it doesn't!" Amelia said. "It's lush, Harold. It's absolutely the most magnificent tail I have ever seen."

"Look, see right here," I said pointing to a spot near the base. "It could fill out quite a bit more here."

"Listen fluffy," King said. "You look great. You'll have more food flying at you than you'll know what to do with."

"Let *me* go!" Sidney said. "We'll do like we did before yeah, and I'll go get the nuts, and I swear, I'll bring you guys back tons."

"Will you show a little pride, please?" King said.

"Pride don't bring home the nuts," Sidney said under his breath.

"Oh look! What a cute little squirrel," a blonde woman said to the man she was with. They stopped walking and she moved slowly toward me so as not to scare me off. He eyes and cheeks were shining and her smile was as lovely as the spring weather. "C'mere little squirrel, come—*ick!*" She straightened up, a sour look spoiling her pretty features. "Rats!" She pointed at King, Amelia, and Sidney. She followed her friend across the street. "Really," she said, "this city has *got* to do something about the rat problem!"

"Ah, your mother!" King swore after them.

We climbed through the hole and into the suitcase, not saying anything more about my tail. Omar was already asleep, and King, Amelia, and Sidney soon joined him. I lay down, but that wonderful smell was reaching down into the basement and making my nose itch. I wanted to see the azaleas, if just for a second. And since I was still awake, well, maybe it was the time.

I felt a little bit shaky as I approached the park. It looked magnificent in its new green suit, and the smell of flowers and tree buds and sap was intoxicating even from across the street. I felt like I was flying through a dream, past the story of Ida and Isidor and the *Titanic*, past the PLEASE DO NOT LITTER sign and the orange wire trash basket. The statue of Memory lay ahead, a field of yellow-and-red striped tulips between us, azalea bushes and ginkgo trees on either side

With a light hollow thud, a big fat macadamia nut hit the ground and split in two right in front of me. I looked up

into the kind, benevolent face of Macadamia, a face that said nothing could be wrong in the world. "Hey there little friend—where have you been? I was worried about you. Did you go south for the winter?" he said, and chuckled to himself.

I had sworn to myself I would never accept another nut from Macadamia, but now that I had the chance to refuse him, I didn't see the point. It seemed a lifetime ago that I was angry at him. Now I just felt sad.

I ate one half of the nut and picked up the other in my mouth and walked back to the basement. I laid it on the middle of the floor and crawled into the suitcase.

I was having a bad dream when King woke me up. "Harold! What is the meaning of this nut?"

"Can't you see?" Amelia said to him. "He went to his park and he brought back some food for us. That was so thoughtful of you Harold."

"Yeff, tho thothful," Sidney said, his mouth full of macadamia.

"So this is it, I guess." King nodded, agreeing with himself. "You're leaving us. Well, I told you it was time to go home."

"But it's not my home!" I said. "I mean, not anymore. Oh, I don't know if I even have a home."

"No home?" King said. "Listen to you: no home! You've got two homes. Everybody should be so lucky."

Amelia was at my side, her arm around me. "He's right Harold. Your home will always be the park, and your home will always be with us too."

"Yeah," King said. "Now stop feeling sorry for yourself and go back to that park and run up and down the trees like a mindless idiot and bury nuts and smell flowers and do all that stuff you've been boring us to tears talking about."

"I don't know," I said. "I mean, I always believed in what that sign in the park said, about love and loyalty and never forgetting. Ida would have never left Isidor just because he went bald. Am I just supposed to forget how mean everyone was if they start throwing me nuts again?"

"You have to understand, Harold, they're just trying to be nice," Amelia said. "They don't know any better than to be mean to a rat, and not so long ago neither did you. Did you go see Macadamia every day because you liked him, or because he had food for you?"

"It was the foods," Omar said, sniffing around.

"I'm sure there were many other nice folks who couldn't afford to keep you in expensive nuts," Amelia said.

"Well, *I* would like to bite that ungrateful old prune on his good leg," Sidney said.

"Sid, you need help," King said, and wolfed down the last crumb of macadamia. "I'll tell you something Harold, these macadamias really are tasty."

Coda

I love it. The bark of the trees, the spring of the branches, the tickle of the leaves as I leap through them, the warm kiss of the sun, the satisfying feel of the soil, and the people. Macadamia, the subway conductor, the lady with the Brazil nuts on Tuesday, and the old man back from Florida, they're all here. New ones too.

Terrence is around too, and we've resumed our sunset conversations. He's fascinated by my adventures as a rat, and he likes hearing about life on the streets. "So how do you tell which lumps are the good ones?" he asks.

I no longer stay in Straus Park all the time. I travel. The places I've visited are: Harlem Meer, a lovely lake in Central Park where I met many nice and well-groomed squirrels; St. John the Divine, the biggest cathedral in the world (or almost the biggest, anyway); Grant's Tomb, which is where President Ulysses S. Grant is buried; and Columbia University, which is a part of the Ivy League, although I looked and could find no ivy there. I even returned to Riverside Park, where, in light of my healthy tail, I was issued an official apology by the Grand Council of the Brotherhood of Squirrels and granted a tourist visa.

All of these places are within walking distance of my park. My big trip is going to be to New Jersey. I haven't quite figured out how to get there yet, but when I do Amelia is coming with me.

I see the rats a lot. I always set aside some nuts for when they come to the park to visit. Once in a while I'll go out for old time's sake and knock over a few trash cans with them. Then there are the afternoons when the lap of Memory is not quite warm or comfortable enough and my nest feels empty, and on those afternoons I walk down the hill toward the Hudson, climb through the hole and down the wall into the familiar darkness, crawl into the suitcase and squeeze between King and Amelia, and go to sleep.

Author's Note

The locations depicted in this book are real, even Black Rock, which sits on 114th Street just west of Broadway. Sadly, the one place that cannot be visited is the Broadway Barbershop, which stood between 103rd and 104th Streets for most of the twentieth century. It closed in 1996, and much of its interior is now held in the permanent collection of the Museum of the City of New York. Mr. K., who ran the shop for fifty years, used to say he was the last barber in America who knew how to give a proper shave.